# Diving the Seamount

# Diving the Seamount

Tom Rapko

iUniverse, Inc.
New York Lincoln Shanghai

**Diving the Seamount**



iUniverse, Inc.

For information address:
iUniverse, Inc.
2021 Pine Lake Road, Suite 100
Lincoln, NE 68512
www.iuniverse.com

ISBN: 0-595-32085-6

Printed in the United States of America

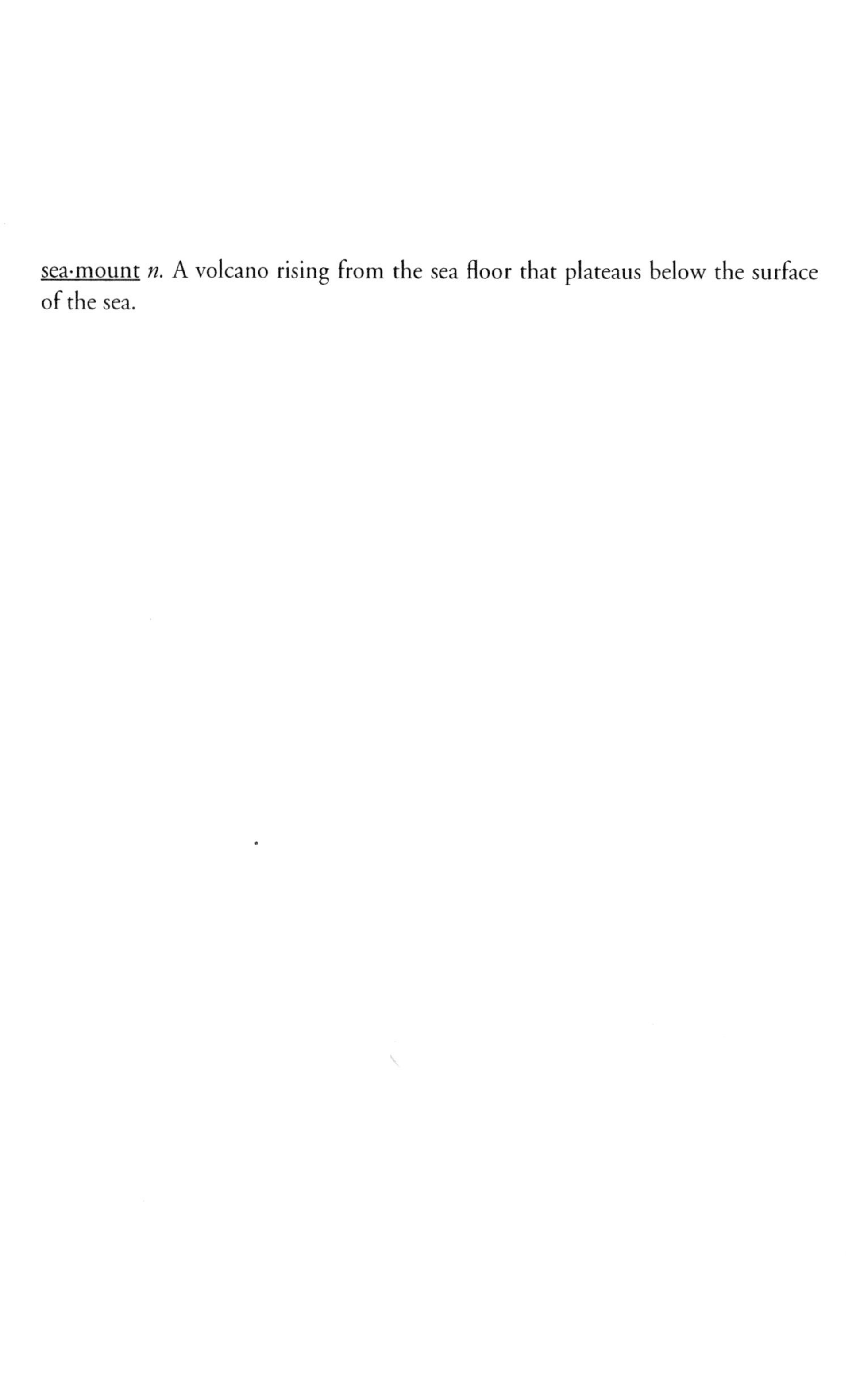

sea·mount *n.* A volcano rising from the sea floor that plateaus below the surface of the sea.

# Chapter 1

It was the dry time of the year in La Paz when morning clouds struggled to survive past dawn. Already the old pearl-farming town, whose pearls had long since been farmed, was stirring. Free range chickens ran from free range dogs and the faucets of a dozen homes tapped into the aquifer.

Slopped over in bed, Pepe heard the kitchen radio playing a Mexican folk song that lingered in the air. He rolled over and slipped his feet down. The cold wood floor creaked in unison with his knees, but the 18$^{th}$ century timbers remained firm. The exterior's stucco, however, was another matter. It needed continual refreshment due to La Paz's exposure to the sea and incessant sun. Pepe, a man afraid of heights, found himself on a ladder more frequently than he wanted.

Like his father, and his father's father, Pepe was a handy-man proud of his instinctive ability to diagnose a problem, find a solution, and fix it. He had modernized much of the old adobe home by copying photos in tourist magazines. Even the bed he was struggling to get out of now had been constructed from a mental blueprint.

He sighed out the bay windows. The morning sun had cat-crawled over the earth and layered the stepped hills in warm skin tones. Not a wisp of moisture appeared in the blue, blue sky. Pockets of vegetation scrambled for real estate with water access. They found it in the moist shadows of fallen stones and under the arms of Socorro cacti. Scrub brush eked out a living by filling in shallow depressions. Higher in the hills trees clung to the sharp stone embankments traversing their sunward path. Contrasting all of this burly vegetation was a seemingly unending sea. It swept across the entire horizon. A big, boisterous blue that had long ago abandoned its innocence now radiated a vibrant aquamarine.

The water rippled as Pepe plunged his hand in and shook his razor. The sink's water was cold, but his razor was sharp so Pepe took long draws. He pinched his cheek to the left, then to the right, and let the tarnished silver blade cut along his throat. It lifted each hair singularly and reduced the scruffy rubble to a soft rosy flush. He moved the blade deftly around his chin and just up to his lips, lips that curled up at the ends into a perpetual smirk. Anchoring all of this was an abrupt nose whose nostrils flared for something more. With a final stroke and rinse Pepe let the silver razor rattle into its cup. He pressed the drain and splashed water along the rim to clean all the little hairs.

A cool desert breeze tugged the curtains and swept full across Pepe's broad back. He stiffened his stance and reached past the chipped wash basin for a beach towel to wrap around his shoulders. Pepe's muscles were those of a manual laborer; toned, lean, and definite. His thighs thinned to molded calves exercised by daily swims. A patch of curly grey hair peppered his chest and served as a throw rug for his fit abdomen. Pepe was to all accounts a handsome man.

He pulled over a t-shirt, slipped on his black swim trunks and made his way downstairs. At the bottom of the stairs Pepe thumbed his dive gear hanging on the stucco wall and took the faded neoprene wetsuit down. He put it, along with the dive vest, fins, mask, and regulators into a worn canvas gym bag. That bag, he thought, somehow survived in better shape than me. Pepe let the bag fly. It slid along the tile floor and settled limply against the door. Pepe reached over a wicker basket filled with tanning guajillo peppers and turned up the radio's volume.

A bean burrito wrapped in tin foil waited for him on the kitchen table. She had been up before him, as usual. He supposed she was already on her morning walk visiting her mother. "Did you ever love a woman" came on the radio and Pepe's mind wandered to when they had met.

She was only sixteen then, propping sunflowers against abandoned gravestones. He had watched her lanky frame unnoticed as she went from grave to grave honoring the dead she couldn't possibly have known in life. Smitten, Pepe rose from the concealment of his parents' gravesite. The mental image of her startled and stumbling over a low-lying fieldstone still made him chuckle. He rarely spent a day without her now, now after thirty years of marriage. It was so easy, and fun, to reminisce about her in the morning. The airy fragrance of her warm, sweet body still lingered in the air. He breathed her in.

A metallic blue arrow shot by the front window. Javier's truck rolled to a stop and dust cascaded past. The well-loved Ford 150 was a staple in Baja, earning its reputation daily on the family farms.

Javier leaned in the doorway with wild horses running in his eyes and his mane flopped over to the left. Three days of not shaving added a certain poignancy to his noise that made his face seem more serious than it really was.

"Hola mi amigo, are you ready to go old man?" Javier scanned the kitchen for something to eat. If Esperenza was here Javier knew for sure he'd get a little something, but pushing Pepe on this never really seemed to work out for him. Pepe offered Javier a seat with the wave of his hand, but Javier nodded him off. He stood fast and feigned indifference to Pepe's chews as each chew corresponded with a growl in his stomach.

Pepe gulped down the last of the fresh orange juice and slid his chair back. He placed the plate into the sink, grabbed his gear and flipped the power switch off as he stepped into the day.

Javier jarred his door open. "You know that girl is driving me crazy." He looked over to Pepe for acknowledgement of his current sanity. The morning always started with two things; the sunrise and Javier recounting his attempts at winning the favors of Mari, the ice cream girl.

"She's a devil that one, oh she may sell frozen candy my friend, but she is a temptress no less." Javier licked his chapped lips and fired the engine.

The truck wheeled around and they bustled down the main boulevard exceeding in degrees each successive speed limit.

Pepe rolled his eyes. "Javier, how long have you been trying for her now? Six months? Seven?"

"Eight months, eight! She doesn't even acknowledge me…and her father…oh he keeps his eye on me more than the gringos!" Javier accelerated the truck out of town with noticeable displeasure. They rickshawed their way along a pot-holed embankment overlooking the marina. Only a handful of boats remained in dry dock now, the majority of the vessels had been in the water for over a month. "Run of Luck," "Feisty Fran," and "The Next Day" dotted the bay, bobbing softly in the breeze.

Pepe breathed deeply and let the morning air fall from its heights onto his lips. He contemplated his words, but decided it was too early for wisdom; as it was Javier was only wearing one sock. He simply mumbled, "Your intentions are too plain."

Pepe cranked down his window. The wind blew his gray hair back. He tried to remember the last time it rained. The parched dirt cracked along the roadside.

When it did rain, Pepe knew it would flood the roads, roads that were left to their own devices. He contemplated the thousand dirt roads that departed from the asphalt; roads that trickled away as only dirt paths but could be seen in the distance heading to a sprawling, fertile ranch or a home perched on the peninsula's shelf commanding a panoramic view of the ocean. The little dirt roads, Pepe thought, those are the important ones to travel.

Javier could tell Pepe was lost in thought about the whole Mari situation, so he counseled his mentor, "She'll give in, they all do. It's just a matter of time old man. You'll see!"

Pepe chuckled first to himself then aloud. "In a month's time you'll be another ten pounds heavier for eating that ice cream and your intentions having advanced no further."

"We'll see, we'll see," rolled from Javier's lips.

"Oh we will, and until then keep the truck on the road," Pepe motioned.

Javier fish-tailed the truck in line. They rambled away from La Paz with their dive gear clanking against the steel bed. The full sun triumphantly passed over the horizon and sat on the arid hilltops.

# Chapter 2

The rich clay felt soft in his hands and ideal for flaming. Cervantes had been using this recipe since opening his shop twenty years ago. Arcilla rica, rich clay; he dug it by hand from coveted clay pits in the Sierra Guadalupe mountain range nestled on the eastern edge of the desolate Vizcaíno Desert. The Vizcaíno Desert, whose only moisture seemed to come from the rolling fogs of the Pacific, somehow yielded the finest clay.

La Paz's profitable tourist industry had just begun then and his hobby was a way to make a couple extra pesos after his retirement from the Mexican Petroleum Corporation. He lived now on his PEMEX stipend and sold pottery to tourists on the side. It was an all together fulfilling use of his time and although Baja Pottery Inc. wasn't particularly notable, Cervantes consoled himself with the thought that nothing in La Paz of its own merit was notable. The combination, however, of its position near Fresh Fruit Ice Cream and the La Paz Inn made it a must-see, must-buy-from attraction for tourists. They bargain hunted along the cracked cement sidewalk snapping about from shop to shop in their rubber flappers.

Cervantes had expanded operations from his original outdoor push-cart by a bit of luck when both the timbers and furnishings of a shipwrecked boat became available to him. He never did find out if the owner of that beached boat wanted them back or not. Fortunately, the collective conscience of the city had long since forgotten the requisition and now there wasn't anything at all particular about either the appropriation or construction of the facility.

The ramshackle building was a lot tougher than it looked, it had even passed the building inspector's rigorous twelve minute examination. Cervantes keep strict business hours, and today was no exception; he would work until something else caught his attention. Just last week he had nearly finished three kitchen pitchers when word came around town that a pinto bean slingshot contest was being organized. Naturally they needed Cervantes to help mediate it. Or was it his idea to organize it from the beginning?

Mariposa's dress fluttered into the shop and before Cervantes saw her he felt her presence. "Hello papa." She leaned over and kissed him on his wrinkled forehead.

Cervantes smiled and breathed deeply of the life she exuded. It had kept him alive for the past decade, and he believed it would last another ten. She tickled men's fancy with her walk and teased their imagination with her smile. Naturally she was unavailable, especially to gringos, and more especially to Javier Vasquez.

"What have you been making papa?" Always "papa" she called him, even now early in her twenties she retained the air of a nymph.

"A fruit bowl Mari. It will be baked this afternoon if I am not drawn into another fisherman's card game. You see how the edges here are fluted? And notice too the texture of this clay?" Cervantes ran his thick, weathered hands along the edge of the bowl. Mari gingerly lifted the bowl from her father's hands. The clay was more ductile than usual; it was slippery even when dry.

"What is it papa?" She rotated the bowl, curious of the texture.

Cervantes pointed into the garbage bin towards a slow-burning lamp. She saw a heap of fruit rinds taken from Fresh Fruit Ice Cream.

"Ah-ha," she giggled. "So you have used some fruit!"

Cervantes' lips parted into a smirk, "fruit oils, butterfly, what better for a fruit bowl?"

# CHAPTER 3

The airline pilots had been driving for over an hour and had already passed two beers out the window. The roadside scenery wasn't the worse for wear though, the trail out of Cabo north was littered with a discernable nonchalance.

"We definitely need to get a group together and drive the length of this drag one day," Jack, the better looking one, said. They whipped across the spider-cracked asphalt.

His co-pilot nodded in agreement, that would definitely be one heck of a trip. Jack lit a cigarette and smacked his lips. "Ahhh Freddy you gotta love this Mexican beer, two for ten pesos!"

"Damn right, it's a heck of place. Everything for sale but nothing worth owning!" Freddy laughed. Freddy had a large freckle above his left eye that seemed to laugh too.

Jack peeled an orange and drove with his knees.

"I got it," Fred steered as Jack finished peeling his orange. He tossed the rind out the convertible Bug's back. It flopped twice then slid unto the road's shoulder.

"I love coming down here to dive. Airline pays us per diem, we get a couple days off, and then back to the real world," Fred's comments fell off-hand.

"Yeah, a couple days are great, but any longer and you're starting to live like the people around here in their stucco homes...eating nothing but beans and oranges." Jack looked down the highway. Orange groves in neat rows ran its length blanketing their sense of smell with a smooth citric air.

"Ain't that the truth...good thing there's beer, because I wouldn't touch the water around here!" Fred popped open another beer and handed it to Jack.

"Cheers Fred, to Baja!" Jack grinned as he passed into La Paz without stopping at the first stop sign, nor the second.

"Cheers mate!" Freddy clicked his can against Jack's. A rusted hulk of a police cruiser pulled behind them.

# CHAPTER 4

Javier wheeled the truck around the building and parked under a row of imported palm trees. This resort was nice. It had all the amenities his countrymen didn't need; a hot tub, swimming pool, and bottled water. Americans paid half his monthly wage for a well-appointed bedroom. The dive shop where he worked was adjacent to the hotel, but for liability reasons not necessarily connected.

"Javier, that new roof is coming along nicely," Pepe talked as he walked. He inspected the new beams and felt the pulled thatch that was going to be the roof. It was thick and tough, home-grown in Baja from Gringo Green, a new plantation dedicated to the organic growth of palm and date trees by some Californians flush with cash.

"The roofers worked on it most of yesterday. I figure we should have some shade over our heads again by the end of the week," Javier fingered over to Pepe showing him the new work. A few black chars still remained on the concrete from the fire. Javier had taken it upon himself to supervise the reconstruction of the roof he had burnt down.

"Who do we have diving with us today?" Pepe asked no one in particular. He ran his fingers down the list of names scribbled in the water-stained log book. It would be eight on the boat today, including him and Javier. Pepe looked across the water. It was flat today. He was confident they could make good time to the seamount. About the same instant Javier found a problem.

"Pepe, the speedboat's engine isn't hitting. I think we've got a problem," Javier grimaced.

Pepe walked over to the speedboat's mooring. Sea Zephyr had the design and power of a racing boat but accommodated scuba divers. They sat with their tanks to her rear, actually strapped their feet to the deck, and basically held on for dear life. Of course no professionally sanctioned scuba diving organization would approve this boat for diving, but then again this was Mexico.

Javier's mechanical skills were on par with his fire prevention skills. Pepe shook his head and stepped onto the boat. He smelled gasoline. The boat rocked in the water and listed against the pier. Pepe checked what Javier was doing. He had managed to remove the engine's cover and was in the process of stripping the bolts out of the intake cylinder's casing.

"Easy Javier! Use this to tighten up the plugs and make sure the connectors are secure, that's where the problem usually is," Pepe handed Javier a socket wrench and guided him over the engine.

Half an hour later it still wasn't working so Pepe decided that this indeed may be out of his hands. He walked back to the shop and dialed up Lisa. Lisa was a regular from Loreto who drove down the coast every couple weeks to dive in La Paz. She was staying at the resort for the night and diving with them, if the engine worked, in an hour. Notwithstanding the fact that she was a good diver, she also owned a service garage and landscaping business in Loreto.

Lisa came down to the shop ten minutes after the call in a pair of sweatpants and a crème tank-top with spaghetti straps. She was forty-eight, thick, and an American expatriate who had made the move to Baja three years ago after a divorce. Baja had succeeded in saving her like so many others.

Emotionally drained, she was waking and walking then only out of habit. Lisa settled for half of half of what she deserved just to move things along; he got away with a new woman and a sizable war chest. At that point it really didn't matter though, for Lisa her marriage had been slowly dying for years, it was like a cancer on her heart. Occasionally, all too occasional, it went into remission, but this was only long enough for him to gain some fortitude to pursue other woman. He was loud and boisterous, which she had first interpreted as courage and character, but his words never could drown out the lasting effects of his actions.

She ended up leaving with her truck, some clothes, and a bank account she could access in Mexico. Lisa always did like seeing her available balance in pesos and the simple fact that most people paid for everything in cash here drastically increased her fortunes. There was something about holding currency in her hand that made it all the more valuable, and therefore much harder to part with. The question that most frequently came to her mind now was not what the price was, but rather what was the value? It changed everything.

"Buenos Dias!" Lisa waved to Pepe and Javier as she walked across sand that was still cool on the soles of her feet. She crossed over the length of the pier.

"Javier, give me that wrench. You know a man's place is in the kitchen!" Lisa winked at Javier who took it upon himself to get steamed up before 8 a.m. He stepped purposefully around Lisa without looking up and waited with Pepe in the makeshift kitchen attached to the dive shop.

"How come you're so smart with tools?" Javier thumbed through his words like a tight pack of gum.

"Necessity," Lisa grunted "is my sister!" She flipped the bolt loose and placed the wrench on the dock. Lisa bent over and peered into the engine block. "Fuel line's loosened up, gonna need one of those plastic ties you've got." Pepe grinned at Javier.

Seven minutes later they drank celebratory orange juice liquored with a quarter bottle of champagne the barman brought over to Pepe.

# CHAPTER 5

The honeymoon was finally here and they were together at last! The flight from Boston last night landed in La Paz late enough for Meghan and Gus, August on his passport but everyone called him Gus, Merit to grab a quick bite to eat at the bar, unpack their things, and roll into bed.

Gus was still asleep. His sandy hair had formed an admirable bed head. She could see the outline of his frame silhouetted through the sheets. She loved to watch him sleep. He took shallow breaths that sometimes lapsed into little snores. All she did then was to change her breathing and his would subside. This was the first vacation he'd been on since they started dating nearly two years ago. Finally she had had it, and they both got certified to scuba dive before the wedding. She imagined this to be the first of many trips; he seemed to silently agree.

Meghan thought the timing of their wedding couldn't have been better. Gus had just been made an associate at Meyer, Stoneham, and Brown LLP; a major rung on the corporate ladder had been climbed. Now each hour he put in would count more to their bottom line.

Gus reached over and rubbed Meghan's back. His hands were strong and eased out the knots in her neck. She sighed. He was happy here, she could tell. He kissed her freckled neck and ran his fingers down her side bumping along the contours of her ribs. Meghan giggled.

"Can you imagine staying here the rest of your life," she implored.

"The rest of my life? Hmmmm...I don't know, I haven't slept like that in years...the air here...can you feel it...it's rejuvenating." Gus filled his lungs with a deep morning breath.

"Silly, you were just exhausted from last night!" Her wide green eyes captured his light blues. Gus set the cup of water he was drinking on the nightstand and let her form fill his eyes. Meghan was athletic and neat; partial to tiger lilies and a die-hard Red Sox fan. Her smile conveyed all of that.

"Yes, that was particularly wonderful...but I'm serious about the air, there's something about it." He pulled her close and threw the sheets over their bodies.

# CHAPTER 6

The rigor mortis horse was not a welcoming omen. The beast had obviously been there for a couple days, so one would think that "they" would have cleaned up the remains. But there he was, lying on his back with his feet in the air and a hairy black stomach bloated to twice the normal size. It was almost comical, save for the feasting vultures.

The photographer arrived in Mexico a week ago from Albuquerque. He planned to do some partying, surfing, and diving. With ten trips in the past three years to his credit this horse thing didn't surprise him at all. It just reinforced the Baja he had learned to love. It could be brutual, it was plainly beautiful, and unlike more civilized places, in Baja he could be free. He had driven down to Cabo for a couple days, but decided to part with his buddy after a rough night of drinking landed his buddy in jail and led him to nearly procure the services of an alcoholically-attractive prostitute. So, all in all, the trip had already had some interesting points. Now the plan was to dive a couple days and camp out on the beach.

Naturally, the photographer captured his experiences on film; his most valuable possessions were the photo logs of his adventures. Presently, he was making his way to the dive shop in La Paz to dive the seamount. If the rumors were true, this was *the* place to dive.

# CHAPTER 7

Mariposa left Baja Pottery and walked towards Fresh Fruit Ice Cream. The day was clear and warm already, so she knew they'd be busy before noon. She slid around the storefront's rear and removed an old skeleton key from under the mat. A siren blared in the distance just as Mari opened the rusted lock.

Mari pushed the door open. It was cut wrong, so she had to push up on it when she opened the store. Inside it was dark and cool and not nearly as inviting as it soon would be. Mari made her way across the entrance to the window shade. The cord went taunt as she pulled up the wood shades. Click. Click. Click. Far along the main drag lights were flashing. Two tall white men got out of a car. More gringos she thought. She liked the way they talked. Mari wanted to go to America desperately and made it a point to ask her father daily about the possibility of going to New York in the fall. She had never seen snow and secretly wondered if it would really hurt her eyes.

She slid the ice cream stations open and switched on the ceiling fan. It hummed softly. Before 8:00 AM the delivery truck stopped in front of the shop and unloaded eight cardboard cartons of fruit. They were lumbering banana boxes hauled around all of La Paz filled with fruit grown on family farms. Nonentities in comparison to the massive agricultural communes in the United States, nonetheless, the family farms collectively produced many thousand tons of fruit annually that principally stayed on the Baja peninsula. The oranges seemed just a bit more sour, as they should, and the lemons sourer still. It was a crispness of flavor absent in the palate of engineered fruits and yes, and yes it was true, occasionally an apple here had a worm.

Mari received the boxes one by one from the delivery man and positioned them in the back of the counter under the faucet. She washed the peaches, pears, apples, oranges, and bananas individually and stacked them on the counter. Cream poured from the handle of her pitcher into the ice cream machine. She went back to the ice chest and removed five trays of ice.

Mari lifted the ice and let it fall into the machine's lap. She pushed the stainless steel button and a soft churning started. It whirled the cream and ice rhythmically. Peels of bananas piled into the rubbish bin. She pulled the skin down delicately not to bruise the fruit. She placed it in the ice cream machine and watched it turn and turn until it became thick. She was careful not to add too much of the cane sugar. Mari dipped a spoon into the bowl and tasted the mixture. Her lips parted into a silent smile as she gazed out of the window towards the sky. Her little girl eyes dilated with the overwhelming blue. Mari closed her eyes and breathed it in.

The air soothed her heart. It was cool on the lips, strangely dry and reminiscent of juniper. Its presence took hold of the sails and made them full. It crested waves and glided gulls. And for Mari, it painted the colors of eternal youth on her cheeks.

# CHAPTER 8

The Mexican cat was an interesting story, or at least Esperenza thought so. The feline pranced ahead of her and stopped here and there to smell the ground. Its tail twitched a curious beat and then went still. A striped lizard dashed across the dirt road and the cat pounced after it. Esperenza shifted the weight of the groceries from one arm to the other and let pass from her lips a warm sigh. It was the sigh of a woman pleased with her life.

Brought up in Mexico City, Esperenza's family migrated to the mainland's coast after her father had gotten in trouble with the police over confusion of a car's ownership. When trouble continued to follow the family her mother decided it was time to leave her father.

She took the family across the Sea of Cortez. Similarities in appearance initially welcomed them, but they had in fact stepped onto another world. A world where poverty still pulled at the purse strings, but it was a different poverty. One could find work here and sustain a meaningful life. There was work for those willing and always something for those who weren't.

Somehow Baja preserved a unique status being geographically separated from mainland Mexico that allowed it to survive, indeed thrive, when the rest of the country stumbled.

The peso was taken here but a commodity exchange was still alive. And any way you looked at it, the living was cheap if you knew where to find lodging, where to find fruits, beans, and where to raise a family. Esperenza's mother knew how and where to do all of these things.

She settled the family in La Paz with few odd looks from the locals. The city had become a segregate home for several generations disgusted with the mainland and in search of a better life. They shared the commonality of all migrants and she found their and her situations were the same.

The daughters went to school when it was still unfashionable for girls, and for that matter women, to be getting an education. They stayed longer and excelled further than their contemporaries on the mainland because they could. Instead of being herded for wives, their educations afforded them positions as school teachers, secretaries, and clerks.

The daughters grew up liberal, determined women who subconsciously wound up favoring barrel-chested and wholly entrepreneurial men that took life squarely by the reins.

Now Christel had become a very, very old woman comfortable in her habits and secure in her soul. She saw her daughters often and smiled upon the blessings of life that only came from enduring its trials. She followed Esperenza's outline for the duration of her eyes' limited focus then eased back into her chair prompted up against the stucco wall.

Esperenza slowed her pace as she neared home. The sun had already become warm and she wanted to shower before gardening. It was a strange custom she followed, but one she followed religiously. The old oak door opened and she placed her groceries on the kitchen table.

She smiled at Pepe's dish in the sink; it was spotless as usual. Esperenza settled herself. She laid her shoes on the waiting mat, stood, and let her curly chestnut hair fall its full length to her waist. Esperenza stacked her morning shopping clothes on the shelf and placed her gardening clothes on the freestanding wall. Already the shower beckoned.

It had taken Pepe the better part of a month to complete the large walk-in bathroom. Puzzle-piece tile fired from Cervantes' shop decorated the walls in a vibrant pattern of the moon. A burning Mexican sun with nine outstretched arms decorated the opposite wall.

Esperenza turned the copper fittings and freed the water from the holding tank hot from the late morning sun. Flush with color from the water she rubbed the soaped facecloth across her body. Steam spiraled from her skin and rose out of the open air windows. A smile pressed on her lips as she let the lather bubble over her body.

# CHAPTER 9

Lisa grabbed a scuba tank by its chrome knob and passed it to Pepe to load on the boat. They had already packed all of the weight belts and were now putting two tanks in for each diver.

The boat stowed more gear than it appeared. Its yellow clapboards opened to reveal a ship within a ship. They slid up, down, and across hosting a tank, a dive belt, or a canister of fuel. Each seat was a disguised compartment, the padding came off and held a diver's personal gear. Even the Captain's fiberglass wheelhouse held a surprise; under and behind the chrome-spoked wheel there was enough room for a green oxygen bottle and full medical kit.

Satisfied with the packing, Javier jumped up from Sea Zephyr and walked along the creaking pier past the dive shop. He had enough time for a quick smoke. He pinched a cigarette in his hand and fired a stick from a cheap book of matches.

Javier blew out the smoke in concentric circles that waffled pensively in the air. His mind focused on his problem at hand, Mari. His eyes followed the smoke. She too had an airy way about her he thought. That initially led him to believe she would be an easy date. Reality had proven otherwise. He knew now he must redouble his efforts, then slowly lost himself in thought. The tobacco lapsed and Javier motioned to flick the cigarette. Instinctively he remembered this was how he had started the first fire. Javier cautiously rubbed it out and stashed the butt in his pocket.

Pepe sealed the bow of the boat. All the tanks and weights along with the full fuel for the trip were loaded. He scanned the length of the pier to the hotel's entrance. A convertible white Volkswagen Bug with a knocking engine puttered up. Two men swaggered out, slung dive bags over their shoulders and made their way over to the hotel registry.

Lisa looked at the hands on her watch. "Pepe, I'm going to grab my gear."

She climbed out of the boat and walked towards the hotel. She smelled Javier's smoke and gave a disapproving shake of her head as she passed. A beach trail wound around the back of the hotel and connected with a fine paved sidewalk inlaid with seashells.

Meghan tied her bikini straps taunt and rolled a sweatshirt over her shoulders. Her wide-brimmed hat was on the wicker dresser along with the sunscreen and metallic sunglasses. Gus was waiting for her by the door with their backpacks. He mentally recounted his packing to make sure they had everything. His wallet was in his fleece, the camera in the backpack along with his towel. Meghan's leather pouch was in there too.

They shut the door and walked downstairs. The walkway looped past a freshwater swimming pool, hot tub, and ended on the bar's patio where a cactus in full heat was blooming pink flowers. Already the kitchen behind the bar was alive. Fried eggs and beans lingered in the walkway's air.

Jack chugged a bottle of water, peed, and left his room without flushing. He wore a party sombrero obtained in Cabo that doubled as a protective day hat. It was looped around his neck with long cotton stays secured by a black plastic fastener. His dive gear wheeled behind him on a pull-bag. Jack stopped at Freddy's door.

"Housekeeping, can I help you?" Jack squealed out.

"Why don't you come in here you little hottie!" Fred snapped back. He pulled open the door and had apparently decided on a bright Hawaiian shirt. A gold cross danged on his hairy chest.

"You ready to go mate?" Jack yawned.

"Yeah, just let me get my gear." Fred reached around the slotted closet door and pulled out his dive bag complete with twenty-seven patches acquired from diving around the world. Fred walked out the door and drug it behind him.

The photographer's journey north hadn't gone as well as planned. The rental car brought him twenty minutes past the airport and then succumbed to whatever illness had killed the horse. A thumb back to the agency revealed no other cars ready for rent, but the owner offered his brother's taxi service to La Paz at a discount. Even though it was the photographer's only choice he told them he needed to consider it.

His camera was the last thing to go in the taxi, and he eyed the driver suspiciously. He wondered why this guy's brother was just coincidently going to La Paz this morning, especially so early? The photographer decided to take things into his own hands and snapped a picture of the driver, just in case something went wrong the police would have someone to look for. Then he thought about what he just thought. The police wouldn't care one way or another. Then he was nervous again.

Lisa opened her door and scanned the room for her bathing suit. She went through her suitcase and couldn't find it. She ruffled through her closet and checked the bathroom, finally she spotted the black one-piece hanging in the far dresser.

She slid off her sweatpants and caught sight of her scar in the mirror. Light pink, it ran from the bottom of her bum, narrowed over the cellulite, then thickened just above her knee. It always found a mirror she thought. She turned away from the mirror, pulled on her bathing suit, and put her terry-cloth sweatpants over it all.

Getting a wetsuit on wasn't easy, the reason why it keeps divers so warm was due to its thickness and snugness. Meghan was realizing this now. She tugged on the shoulders to lengthen the arms. Now the zipper wouldn't match up. In a contortionist improv, she doubled over and freed up some room. This would work for her.

"That was the hardest part Meghan, trust me! I'll give you a medium BC…try this mask on…what size are your feet?" Pepe placed the top and bottom in a dive bag for her.

"Where're you from?" Javier kept the conversation light in the morning and relaxed it even more as the day drew out.

"Oh we just flew in from Boston last night." Gus swung the dive vest over his shoulders, adjusted the straps, and put it on his back.

"How close is that to New York?" Javier wondered.

"About five hours north…depending on the time of day," Gus estimated.

Meghan pushed all of her dive gear into the bag and headed over to the boat. She heard the "clank, clank, clank" of wheels on the pier and looked down. Two men, one sombrero, were making their way towards the boat. They waved at Pepe.

"You want our gear on this boat?" Jack pointed over to Sea Zephyr.

"Sure. Swing back here to sign some release forms when you're done, I'd hate to be liable for you two." Pepe winked at them as they passed below and sipped from an overflowing glass of orange juice in his hand.

Lisa packed all her gear and left her room. She turned her head at the blaring Latino music coming from the taxi swerving into the parking lot. The car skidded to a halt. A clean-cut young man jumped out. He grabbed his bag, camera, and before the car door was shut the taxi pulled away and turned up the radio.

"Hi," the photographer shook his head at the departing taxi. He took one look at Lisa's gear. "I guess I can follow you to the dive shop?"

"You sure can," Lisa smiled. She slung her gear bag around her shoulders and headed over to the shop.

In ten minutes this gaggle of divers had loaded their gear into its respective compartments, sub-compartments, and hidden shelves. Pepe greeted his divers gregariously. He turned the ignition key and the engines roared to life. Sea Zephyr's smoky fumes softened to clear exhaust and slowly, calmly, the dive boat eased away from the pier.

# Chapter 10

Cervantes placed his fruit bowl aside, took off his fake turtle shell glasses, and looked at the dozen teacups ready to fire. They were a unique set commissioned oddly enough by Hector Vasquez, the PEMEX Baja president. Making these teacups hadn't been easy. Cervantes needed to replicate a set whose only semblance was derived from a family album. Cervantes had studied the pictures intimately for hours to ensure he had all the right dimensions.

He discerned the pattern, but the original color scheme would have to be an interpretation. The black and white photos never knew that secret. Vasquez told Cervantes to use his judgment and Cervantes took his direction with a tinge of satisfaction. Having his artistic abilities held in such high esteem by a man as powerful as Mr. Vasquez was nothing less than a source of pride for him.

Cervantes had considered using a floral coloring pattern but decided against it; eight rose-hued teacups would be too floral. He thought about pressing ahead with a conservative blue but judged that to be too conservative. Finally Cervantes had found a taste and smell, a whole sensation, that he wanted to impart on the teacups.

As always, the origin of his idea was unique and this too was no exception. He had been walking in the morning as he was apt to do and passed the exterior of Pepe's adobe home, which he noted needed some painting. Always observant, some said prying, Cervantes also noticed smoke coming from the bathroom window. He rushed over to find it was only shower steam. Satisfied that nothing was wrong Cervantes started back towards the road when he smelled the most wonderful smell. It was as if little mangos floated in the air and danced around his noise. He couldn't help himself. Cervantes approached the window and breathed deeply. The soapy perfume mesmerized him. This alone might not have influenced his teacup decision but by opening his eyes he saw the most wonderfully toned skin being lathered. He fell backward in awe, in a stupor of excitement. Mango it would be!

# CHAPTER 11

The sun glistened on the water's surface and echoed beneath the waves. It was too early for them to put the throttle in full, so Pepe let Sea Zephyr idle by the buoys near the steel PEMEX storage tanks. Sea mist foamed in their wake and engulfed little pockets of water.

Long billed avians shot from the sky fishing for sunning minnows. They circled, circled, and dove from the sky piercing the shimmering water and spearing the fish. Rarely, but occasionally it did happen, their angle of attack was too sharp; those were the broken-neck carcasses beachcombers found on the deserted shores.

Everything seemed so alive, so passionate in Baja. Every action had a purpose, instinctively calculated, and executed perfectly. An animal's life depended on it. To fail in the wild was to die, and generations of that upbringing in Baja had led to a streamlined evolutionary process. Divers unaccustomed to this environment experienced a drastic change in perspective; suddenly they realized they weren't necessarily on the top of the food chain.

The divers passed outside the cautioned area and left the last semblance of civilization just ten minutes from the resort. Now the air had a particular laugh of its own, a smile of freedom and irascibility about it. Dual 125-hp engines fired and launched the boat on the crests of the little dimple waves.

The coastline was unaltered and raw. It cut in when it was tired and swooned when the waves came upon it too fast. They approached and passed a white-caped rocky point that had been repeatedly bombed with guano. It now served as the nesting ground for hundreds of fishing birds. Secluded outcroppings dotted the coast and as the view from the rocks fell, dunes arose. Dunes, upon dunes, rolled out from the beach and sprouted green sea grass. Further afield the grass receded, dropped into scrub brush, and finally layered into the classic Baja xenosphere.

Not a ripple cut the water as the boat sped past. Pepe hung out his hand and felt the spray. It was warm and delightful. Simply touching it reminded him of all the dives he had taken here. It was premature for the chatter that would come, so everyone sat still in contentment. Ahead an island came into view. It jutted above the waterline and crested two hundred feet in the air. A flock of old gulls sat perched on its spires. They were talkative, chirping and swirping as the boat approached.

Sea Zephyr came within earshot of the island. Guttural sea lion chugs snapped the silence. The dreamy veil of serenity lifted and the group awoke. A colony of sea lions had marked their ground and lay upon it like princes. The bulls pushed and tugged their way onto the rocks, defecated, hunted, and mated. The females evaded the males and cared for their little pups. As for the pups, the world was theirs. Too young to bark and too little to care they pierced the water's surface with well-timed bounds from the rocks. One swam towards the boat with a knowing spark in his eyes, dipped underwater, and reappeared back at his rock. Pepe veered the boat away and pressed on along the coast.

Concentric volcanic cones rose from the shoreline into the air. The geothermal activity had been, until recently, caustic. The passage of several thousand years had succeeded only in hiding what was already there. Spewing volcanoes took a break and steamed in slumber on the roof of the southern peninsula. Truckloads of thick, rich black ash affixed itself at the base of these spent volcanoes. The rocks were precipitous and needed, it seemed, only a gentle nudge to coming crashing into the water. Only the birds in the air and lizards scampering on the sand added a hint of life to the island.

After two hours Pepe felt, rather than saw, where he was. He eased the throttle back and slid the engines into idle. The sun was high enough and the water calm enough to gaze into the depths. Satisfied with what he saw, Pepe threw the anchor overboard. Clangs softened to the sound of nylon slipping on fiberglass.

Below them was the seamount, a volcano that had plateaued just below the surface of the sea. Its position over a thousand meters from the shoreline and flanked on all sides by excessive depth made this underwater island an oasis. Warm currents played upon its plateau and pollinated it with coral polyps. They affixed themselves to the rocks and attracted hungry juvenile fish. The food chain simply spiraled upward from there.

# CHAPTER 12

An interesting thing happens when you bring together people of different backgrounds, but of shared interest. A pecking order is established. Maybe not official, but a sense, a feeling, of who's who permeates the group. They had talked amongst themselves and to each other up until now only cautiously.

Sea Zephyr anchored and for a moment there was a feeling of awkwardness. Pepe saw it daily and liked how in the morning the group would be reserved and by the second dive together they acted like a family. Pepe moved around the boat handing out gear, adjusting straps, and helping the divers suit up. This was the first part of bringing the family together, equipping them.

"Good morning everyone, I hope you enjoyed the trip out to the seamount." Pepe straddled the bowline. "This morning looks fantastic. This is going to be a wonderful dive, I can tell already."

Javier ran his hand along Sea Zephyr's chrome guardrails as he spoke with a heavy Spanish accent. "If you would please keep the boat steady by having an…" A pod of dolphins shot under the bow and broke the surface of the water. Excited heads followed the splashing.

"What type of dolphins were those?" Gus shouted to Javier.

"Hey can we get in the water with them?" Jack and Fred were putting on their masks to take a peak under the water and see if any more were coming up. The photographer hadn't been caught off-guard. Too many missed shots in his brief career had taught him a lesson. He was at the bow of the boat with four pictures shot before the rest of the people knew what happened. It was always a matter of anticipating what was going to happen, and taking a picture of that. Predictive awareness, that's what he called it.

"Bottlenose dolphins and a nice sized pod of them, seem to be running a school of fish," Lisa spoke as she pulled her hair back.

"Yeah, they're playful, and smart. Their games are teaching the young ones how to hunt. They chase fish up the seamount and cluster them in a food ball," Pepe explained while making an imaginary ball held between his hands.

"The dolphins will corral the fish into a position they can't escape as a group, individually they could escape, but the school mentality now becomes their downfall. The dolphins will eat until their dolphin tummies are full." Pepe rubbed his tummy. He eyed the surface of the water. The dolphins had pushed ahead of the boat and clustered the ball of fish a hundred yards away. The surface of the water rippled.

The gulls off-shore made a beeline for the commotion; they too would eat well. The sky was soon filled with a plume of feathers. Pepe brought the focus of his divers back on the dive despite the ensuing feeding frenzy.

"Javier is going to stay on the boat and I'll show you what's in this beautiful sea." Pepe continued handing out dive gear as he talked to the group.

"What else do you think we're going to see Pepe?" Meghan moved in closer to the center of the boat and rolled her wetsuit halfway up her full bikini.

"The seamount has much life, but better action...nothing routine here, nothing half-speed, and nothing mild." Pepe put his hand on Meghan's head for balance and signaled Javier for the white plastic board. Javier leaned over the steering column, pulled out the plastic board, and tossed it the remaining three feet.

"Native Indians knew about the seamount, but local fisherman rediscovered this site by accident only sixty years ago." Pepe drew with a water-erasable marker as he talked and shortly he had made a relief map of the seamount. "It was subsequently marked and quietly forgotten for another four decades until dive boats had started to search the sea for places to dive. Right now, we're on the seamount's southern tip...need to descend along the anchor line," Pepe started the dive brief. "Seamount tops out at 80 feet...right here," Pepe indicated on the map. "Form up as a group, press around the seamount's bank...coral outcrops along the westward ledge...a spectacular cavern here," Pepe took the marker and drew a concave arc on the board in black. "An air pocket formed when lava cooled and left a shelf open. We'll continue along this wall...watch your depth gauges here as we'll be descending to over 120 feet. Find a reference in the water and stay with it. The best part of this dive is what's going on around you, and in particular, above you."

# CHAPTER 13

Cervantes placed a heap of juniper wood in the kiln. It was old, dry, and brittle. Its experiences had led it in many directions, but it survived and even prospered in the austere desert conditions—just like him.

He mixed the wood and a handful of sea salt into the kiln's heart. Cervantes lit it with a pile of confetti paper he had collected after Cinco de Mayo. More and more confetti paper was tossed under the juniper branches until they spiked warm red then an intense blue. The sea salt crackled. The fire burned and burned.

Cervantes waited patiently for the better part of an hour until a bed of coals had formed. He stoked the coals with the striker and tossed a handful of sea water on them. His shop steamed like Esperenza's bath.

Cervantes cleaned a mesh firing tray and spread light paraffin on the edges. The teacups had been prepared and now were ready to feel the kilning process that would transform the hand-washed and pressed clay into Baja pottery. He arranged the cups on the tray and slid them into the kiln.

The paint had dried moist and he immediately noticed an interesting reaction occurring. The cups flamed on the surface. Instinctively he made to remove them, but wisdom held his hand. He let the teacups settle. The moisture freckled with flames for several moments longer but built their hue in the kiln.

He looked at the wall clock and cycled in his mind how many turns and glazes needed to be done. A loose piece of paper appeared in his hand and he wrote numbers that looked like symbols down on the paper with a thick, hand-sharpened pencil. Kilning the pottery was just as delicate, more so he thought, as preparing fine cuisine. And each of his receipts was unique.

# Chapter 14

Esperenza slapped out the final shirt. Pepe's collared shirtsleeve dive shirts all hung on the hemp line along with several of her floral print dresses. With the sun fast approaching midday they soon would be dry. Indeed, by the time the sun rose to its full height water became vapor almost instantly; there was no mosquito problem because there was no stagnant water problem. Precious fresh water lived only in the city's deep aquifer; there was no river or damn providing limitless irrigation. Only the deep aquifer.

In the old days a well was the only source of tapping the aquifer. The old-timers still relish the memories of their youth when it was a privilege being sent for water because it meant they could have the first drinks of the cool, some said slightly sweet, liquid. As time passed and the city expanded the aquifer needed to be drilled deeper and not left exposed to the elements. So the federal government came in and established a modern water system in La Paz.

Esperenza reminisced about the ease in which water flowed to her garden now. She had built up strong arms and a healthy endurance as a young girl fetching water for her mother. She emptied the wood clothespins in a cloth bag and slid the bag under the patio. Esperenza untied her hat, slipped it off, and passed her guajillo peppers on the way.

They were drying nicely on the breakfast table and would make a fine powder when done. She moved across the kitchen and pulled the white curtains open. A string of butterflies danced into the room. They frolicked in the shade and smelled the kitchen's cut flowers. They loitered for a moment, laughed to themselves, then hang-glided towards the garden where drinking droplets still glistened on the leaves.

Sometimes they came in the afternoon. Groups of them arrived with the warm breeze, loitered as they were prone to do, then disappeared to wherever butterflies disappear to. Esperenza looked through the window into her garden and saw them approach from the hills. It was too cool for them near the water during the night and too warm when the sun crested at noon, but now, now, it was perfect.

They were vibrant monarch princesses with wings as large as a child's hand. They fluttered in the air and one by one perched on a clump of cactus blooms, tickled the stamens with their antennae and feasted on the sweet nectar. The sorority of butterflies teased the cactus for a bit longer then thought less of it and left for a flowering pepper. Here they congregated for a great while in butterfly time and seemed to discuss the events of the day. Esperenza waved to them like her sisters and continued to husk the half-dozen ears of corn she purchased at the market.

The butterflies collectively nodded in agreement, sprang from their pepper perches, took to gallivanting the skies again. Esperenza shucked the last ear and swept the husks together with her hands into a neat pile on the countertop. She felt the temperature of the peppers. Satisfied, she grouped the long-stemmed pointy red peppers closer together and made room for herself at the table. She opened her leather-bound notebook and continued writing down the stories her mother told her as a girl.

# Chapter 15

Six batches of ice cream had been mixed and set in the display case. Mari glanced over her work and was relieved to be done before the siesta crowd came for their ice cream. Her apron's knot unraveled as she loosened the ties and grabbed the washcloth hanging from the counter.

Mari cleaned the tile top and polished the wood façade of the counter. All that was needed now was to open the striped red, green, and white awnings. She gathered together the last of the utensil sets wrapped in napkins and placed them in the hostess drawer. The first patter of customers' feet wouldn't be long off.

# Chapter 16

Six splashes were followed by a seventh. Lisa back-rolled into the sea and slowly recovered. Her inflated vest cushioned the aluminum tank's shock.

"Hey Freddy can you turn on my air?" Jack asked from the water. A slightly embarrassing realization made before a much more embarrassing decent was made. Freddy swam over and turned the rubber knob counter-clockwise until it stopped, then rolled it back a quarter turn.

The photographer had entered the water first and had his camera handed to him. It became obvious to the casual observer that underwater photography was far more complicated than it needed to be. The industry was waiting for its equivalent of the disposable camera.

As it was, two arms were connected to a base plate that held a camera-inside-a-camera; a shell of hard plastic had been constructed around a decent 35 mm camera body and sealed via plastic o-rings and silicon grease. In addition to the arms, the camera also had a subset of lenses attached that could either capture wide angle photography for the expected hammerheads or a macro lens in case the dive turned out to be a wash. It was an overly complicated set-up for a seemingly simple product.

Gus and Meghan were doing fine. They had slipped over after Pepe so he could watch them if anything went wrong. Despite their inexperience Pepe felt comfortable taking them on this dive. He paired them together and would keep them in close visual range. With Lisa in the water the group was complete. They made their way to the anchor line.

Pepe raised his right hand in the air and gave the thumbs down signal. Exhaust valves released the air in their vests and the divers felt their bodies sink. They descended along the anchor line past twenty, then thirty, and forty feet. The water was temperate and gushy. Depth compressed the effective thickness of their wetsuits, so with each descending foot the water would become that much cooler. The water aerated with bubbles. Time slowed. The nylon anchor line glimmered upwards like a long, thin strand of tinsel. Phosphorescence in the water added to the natural light providing the divers with a distinct impression they were engulfed in St. Elmo's fire.

The seamount grew large before their eyes. It enveloped all the earth below them and was encircled by a deep, dark abyss. The divers added air to their vests to slow their descent. Their vests filled and eased their fall. Pepe tweaked his vest and effectively became weightless, each diver in turns followed suit. A swarm of glittering fish flashed by their path. They had descended upon El Dorado.

The volcano's electromagnetic force attracted species not normally found off of the coast. It was like this at all areas of intense volcanic activity that afforded shallow enough seamounts to dive. It attracted, spawned, and brought out the strengths of a species. Whatever their life force naturally was, the seamount amplified it. Sponges fixed tightly on the rock outcroppings grew denser and larger than their Caribbean counterparts. Their coral matrix was crisp and durable. The clarity of the water allowed the sun's rays to penetrate deeper and nourish life. A dizzying array of cubic, triangular, and spiral plankton self-illuminated themselves. Petite jellyfish pulsed gently in the current. Streams of yellow-banded amberjack swam towards the divers.

They took long, deep breaths from their tanks and scanned the water around them. The plateaued summit stretched for the length of a football field and a width half as long. Sharp stints and shallow depressions layered the terrain. The divers fanned out in a loose delta behind Pepe.

Pepe tilted his head back and checked the divers behind him. He canted his head toward his chest and let a rattle of air pass between his lips. His kicks were deliberate and smooth, propelling him just where he always wanted to be. His gauges and equipment had somehow fused to his body like an extension of his wetsuit. He was silk underwater and little fish looked toward him for encouragement.

Fourteen fins kicked with the thermal waters that rose from a slight fissure on the seamount's surface. The water seemed lighter here. Perhaps the magnetic field repelled heavy particles or the seamount's summit still exhausted air from the center of the earth. Whatever the cause, when the current was slack it formed a thick, gelatinous thermocline which kept the seamount several degrees warmer than the adjacent water. Some said this was the reason that hundreds of juvenile fish made the seamount their nursery.

The divers' air cascaded upwards and billowed up on the surface allowing Javier to track them. They kept together in a loose gaggle of swaying arms and bobbing heads. Pepe motioned with the index finger of each of his hands held parallel for the group to follow him. He dipped under a rift and led the divers through a cave that had formed a thousand years ago.

A crack in the ceiling illuminated the cavern. Teeming lobster eyes reflected back dots of light. Antennae dusted the water searching for some feel of food. The divers lurched out of the cave and followed the shelf. It dipped to 95 feet. And that is when they saw them. Above the divers swam scalloped hammerhead sharks. The sharks seemed almost frozen in the current, only moving their fins slightly to adjust their position in the water. Their slanted heads swung side to side as the divers came to their level.

The hammerheads were twelve foot primordial beasts with blue suits of scales that suspiciously eyed these intruders on their domain. A fully equipped scuba diver was, fins to head, a comparable-sized animal to the hammerhead. The apex predator felt the cold chill of challenge run down its cartilage.

A bright flash illuminated the water, then another. The photographer pressed closer to the sharks. His breathing slowed to a stop. Thumb to knob, fingers to strobe he adjusted the camera and let the sharks come to him. They stalked the divers for a moment longer, then purposely descended below the divers toward a destination below where they hunted fish with keen magnetic sensors in their hammerheads.

The divers swam past the seamount's jagged rim into blue water; water that had no discernable bottom. It was eerie for them hearing only the sound of their own breathing echoed back to them. They breathed deeper from the aluminum tanks knowing they had entered a kingdom unlike any they had ever seen before.

Its richness was its emptiness from the material world above. Diving in the deep blue reinforced the desire to live, to grow, to expand. They felt it. Here they were simultaneously the stars and planets. The pettiness of life dissolved in the water around them. It was swept away and all that was left was breathing. Deep, fulfilling breathing.

Pepe looked at his dive gauge. He motioned around the group to examine theirs. The divers displayed their air pressures to Pepe. He took the time to examine each diver's gauge and satisfied with his investigation he made the motion to surface.

They added air to their vests and slowly ascended, foot by slow foot, from 120 feet to 30 feet. They hovered in the water motionless, cogniscent they were completely helpless from whatever was in the deep blue below them.

They breathed and bubbled and smiled somehow amongst themselves. The photographer checked his watch and saw only forty minutes had expired in the mental lifetime that they had just spent diving the seamount.

After lingering at fifteen feet for three minutes the divers surfaced one by one. They inflated their vests and floated. Regulators dropped from their mouths and the compressed air was replaced with a warm, salty sea breeze. The divers slow-kicked on their backs towards the waiting boat with the luxury one has of having all the time in the world.

In the distance the divers heard Sea Zephyr's engines come to life. They plodded along the surface, squinting from the noon sun blazing above them. The engines grew louder then knocked off. Far in the distance the sea slapped against the desert shore. Only occasional dots of green could be discerned on the land.

A strategically knotted thirty foot nylon rope fell across the water. "Grab a hold of the line!" Pepe motioned as he pulled himself up on the boat. Pepe unfastened his dive gear and handed it up to Javier. The boat drifted in the current. The divers grabbed the line and leisurely pulled their way onto the boat. Diving was never meant to be a fast sport; slow, deliberate movements define it—there was far too much equipment to move quickly!

Tank after tank danged against Sea Zephyr. Javier stacked them in the aft storage area. He readied the boat for the divers leaving the water. A towel was waiting on each seat along with a cool drink. Some of the group took off their wetsuits and draped them over the side of the boat. The sound of carbonated soft drinks opening filled the air. When they were settled, Javier handled the boat over towards the beach.

# CHAPTER 17

Cervantes peeked inside the kiln. The tea cups were firing nicely. The paint had flared differently on each cup. One was shiny and reflective, another took on an air of relaxation. He closed the kiln door with a nudge. The ash base was large enough to finish the batch.

In between a stack of books and a vintage bottle of Tequila there was a box full of seashells. Cervantes had found most of them along the shore, but occasionally he played the fisherman in games of cards for beautiful shells. It was an old man's adage to risk a little for something beautiful. He pulled the wood box closer to him. Behind it was a stack of cards. Cervantes reached for them. The siesta was the young man's time for love, it was his time for cards.

# CHAPTER 18

The tethered anchor slapped softly against the surface and fell still after just an instant. "OK everyone we're here for our lunch!" Javier announced. He grabbed a cooler and gave it to Pepe who was already in the water. He floated the plastic cooler behind him as he waded toward the beach.

The beach was magnificent in nakedness. Not a trace of man was apparent; there were no footprints nor trash, indeed the only sign of life was an occasional bird's whistle. It was a fine sand beach whose mounds were white and speckled with seashells. The seven divers and Javier swam the short distance from the boat to the beach and laid their towels on the sand as makeshift pillows. The group had already thrown themselves into wild discussion about the dive on the boat ride over, they continued it here with the most intriguing topic being the presence of the hammerhead sharks.

Freddy scratched the sand with a stick illustrating the shark he saw. "It had a large imposing dorsal fin, almost straight up, not slanted at all."

The photographer looked at the caricature and laughed. "No it's not quite that obtuse, it crests at the tip there." He tossed a pebble on the drawing indicating where he meant. "I must have a picture or two of the fellow that I can show you."

"Maybe from the rear," Jack laughed, knowing the kid had only taken shots as the sharks were swimming away from them.

"Pepe, are there whales around here too?" Meghan wondered.

Pepe gave an ironic smile and looked over to Lisa. She had peeled off her wetsuit now and the scar on her thigh throbbed pink.

"That's how I got this actually," Lisa said as she looked over to Pepe and Meghan. "I was free-diving," Lisa slowed her story so the food stuffing of Jack and Freddy subsided "in La Paz almost two years ago when this happened." She glided her finger along the crooked length of the scar. Like all scars, it puffed when exposed to salt water. Lisa pulled back her dirty blonde hair and tied it in a pony tail with the elastic around her wrist.

"Pepe had a group of us out here. I was swimming along when I saw a black shadow rise from the sea floor. It grabbed me by my leg. I couldn't' break free." Lisa spoke with the rare calmness possessed by those who have felt the presence of death.

The tertiary conversations on the beach stopped and focused, even if they seemed not to be, on Lisa. She held out both of her landscaper's hands and indicated the jaw position of the whale. A grim outline followed along her buttocks to the crest of her knee.

"He took me down beneath the waves. My ears exploded as he descended. I didn't have time for a breath before the whale took me. My heartbeat spiked...I remember it getting dark around me, the whale must have sensed that I wasn't going to make it to wherever he was taking me. I couldn't move. Everything around me was black and my body went limp. He swam back up to the surface, released me, and Pepe says waited until Sea Zephyr plucked me out of the water."

The group fell silent. "Well, I can't touch that one by a long shot!" Jack started with a snap in his lips.

He, along with the rest of the group sat quiet for a second trying to comprehend what Lisa had experienced. The silence held their thoughts and after more than a respectful time passed questions blazed again. First to Lisa then slowly shifting to Pepe as Lisa deferred to him more and more.

How long had he been diving here? Would he ever leave? All the while Gus had been lost in his own world. Pepe saw this change overtake people quite often. It was the conversion of a clock-watcher to a life-liver. It was natural in his world. Hammerheads swam by the rich and poor, whales kissed who they pleased, and Gus began to internalize what it meant to be alive. Gus scanned the sea and seemed to have reached some quiet epiphany. He found himself in that classic case of manhood where reflection on a certain subject had drowned out all realization of what was occurring around him. Gus thought life for many seemed to be only a delayed promise, whereas for a fortunate few they simply lived their dreams.

Meghan nudged off from Gus and was gathering up seashells in her damp t-shirt. She walked along the shore barefoot as the bait fish dashed away from some predator and showered the shallows with sprinkles of light. Her eyes scanned the shore for something that could cement her memories to this land. Half-buried in the sand in front of her was a paper nautilus shell. Its delicate, white-ribbed structure had survived the passage from the sea to land largely intact. It only needed to be rinsed to illuminate its beauty. Meghan held it in her hand and dusted the sand away.

The photographer too had gone for a stroll and had positioned himself in a field of jagged, waist high sea grass that cut each of his steps. He struggled to get out of it. Prickly seconds turned into minutes until at last he reached his destination, a lone saguaro cactus upon the ridge.

It was an ancient specimen that had been growing there for centuries. The base was solidly two arm lengths in circumference and sprouted three spires from its stump. Marooned in the sand, the cactus devoured all of the water from the sky above it. Little birds nested in its peak. The photographer took his time and let film capture the beauty of this idol.

# Chapter 19

A steady beat of feet made their way to Fresh Fruit Ice Cream. Mari pushed the scooper deep into the container and felt the metal scrape the edge. There had been more customers than she could have dreamed today. Ice cream melted in people's stomachs faster than in the sun. They were lined up behind the counter like gunslingers of yesterday wanting their tequila.

"Mari my dear, how is that crazy father of yours?" The question came sternly from a commanding voice.

Mari raised her head level to the eyes of Mr. Vasquez. He was on his lunch siesta and never failed to stop in and see her. He was oily, thick in the neck, and flat-footed to a fault. She tolerated him like most women tolerate men who play on their charms; well.

"Papa is crafting some commissioned work," she tapped out the last scoop of mango banana ice cream into a child's paper bowl.

Not to be dissuaded by the number of customers in line before him, Mr. Vasquez continued his direct line of questioning and solidified his inability to see the obvious. He had been steadily promoted up the chain at PEMEX with such alacrity for identifying nothing new and streamlining processes that had become obsolete.

He was one of many new guard janissaries that had entered the workforce and helped modernize Mexico into a prime supplier of cheap goods to the United States. His efforts had not gone in vain. Some three hundred former independent farmers and ranchers had agreed to sell their land stakes to PEMEX with the understanding that they could get quality work at the plant. Naturally then, he was proud of his work and wanted to share the industrial idealism with Mari.

# Chapter 20

Sea Zephyr churned the water in concentric circles then sped off away from the beach. Its warm sands baked in the afternoon sunlight. The divers plopped over the thick waves. Sea Zephyr instinctively motored back to the seamount for their second dive. The mood was boisterous and gay; the divers had filled their bellies, laid in the sun, and now were chattering about the dive ahead.

Morning calmness was replaced with growing waves and a slight current. Javier slid along the fiberglass floor until he jutted up against the cross-support. He unfastened the anchor and was thinking of letting her slip when Pepe approached.

"Javier, let's try a drift dive this time...around the eastern slide of the seamount. I've got the signaling buoy with me I can inflate." Javier saw the inflatable orange tube Pepe was talking about. He silently agreed, the water wouldn't hold for a set dive. Javier moved back behind the Captain's wheel and waited until the divers were suited up. Javier shook his head with a sarcastic smile, it always took them twice as long after lunch.

"What type of film are you using?" Jack was a bit of a photographer and was seriously considering getting into underwater photography.

The photographer pulled a roll from the inside strap of his black photo bag and tossed it over to Jack.

"I like to use 400 speed film, it gives me more flexibility in the shots I can take."

"Hmmm...good stuff, see you have a macro lens too," Jack indicated with the tip of his finger.

"Yeah, picked that up last year, tell you, the best investment I ever made for this camera. I could spend a whole dive just taking pictures of the small things, a whole dive in a five foot by five foot block. We get carried away with trying to see everything sometimes." The photographer reached out for the roll of film. His last comment hadn't gone unheard. Pepe looked at the young man and appreciated his wisdom.

The group was ready to go. They watched Pepe signal Javier to bring the boat around to the eastern half of the seamount. The sun was positioned perfectly to illuminate the depths without reflecting the water's glare. Even with the soft waves it was possible to see schools of fish grouping below the boat.

Pepe gave the overboard signal and the divers back-flipped into the water, except for Meghan who caught her fin on the center seat. She was dangling precariously upside down, half underwater and half above. Her arms splashed "help!" Pepe immediately saw what had happened and signaled Javier to cut the engine power. Javier bounded over to the center of the boat. He clicked the quick-release strap and plopped Meghan into the water.

The waves splashed her head-over-heels in a rolling backflip that ended with her bopping on the tops of the warm ocean mass.

"Ha, you better take this with you...it is very difficult to dive with one fin!" Javier winked as he removed the fin trapped under the seat and tossed it over to Meghan.

The seriousness of the commotion subsided into laughter. Everyone double-checked his gear. The divers grouped together. Gus made sure the rest of Meghan's equipment was ready to dive. Sea Zephyr kicked out leaving the divers hovering directly above the seamount more than a kilometer away from the arid shoreline.

The divers mouthed their regulators. Air fizzed from their vests. Jack and Freddy opened their exhaust valves and sunk like the lead weight around their waist. Only a stream of bubbles identified they had been there. The photographer adjusted his camera. He turned the yellow flash knob to "on" and affixed the macro lens underwater to avoid air reflections in the pictures. Lisa dumped all her air and was in quick pursuit of the pilots. Gus and Meghan descended in tandem looking at their gauges noting both the dive start time and depth. Pepe positioned himself between the extremes.

From the blue shadows a manta ray glided along flapping its wings. It took graceful, deliberate sweeps as it cruised by the divers. The ray's white belly had two emerald remoras cleaning it. The manta made another pass and opened its wide skimming mouth toward a spot in the water filled with plankton.

A flash illuminated the water, there was darkness again for a moment, then another flash burst came. The manta posed thoughtfully, for it is a noble creature, and then made way to the next spot of plankton.

Meghan let her eyes fall on the seamount below. She stabilized her descent and fanned above the water. She heard the crackling of a parrot fish eating coral. Its beak-shaped buck teeth and tropical coloration made it easy to identify.

Pepe signaled with a closed-fist to some point in the distance. Ahead of the divers two green eels had wrapped themselves in a mating ball. The photographer ignored the warning and kicked toward the green ball—and that is generally what separates Mexico scuba diving from anywhere else in the world; the lack of control the divemaster was willing to exert. It was a freedom experienced on many levels, but best typified in this instance as the photographer rushed back to the group with two large green eels in hot pursuit.

Jack and Freddy had abandoned the main group when they found a friend. He jetted away from them initially, but now they had the octopus cornered in a rocky crevice. Jack signaled to Freddy what he was going to do. He moved around the side and removed his plastic snorkel. He prodded the edge of the crevice and the octopus, who is nobody's fool, eased out.

In one of those rare instances where man was faster than animal, Freddy grabbed the octopus. Or it should be said he grabbed it first because its tentacles instantly had his arm wrapped. Freddy immediately learned the adage that there is no weak wild animal. The three foot octopus clamped down on his arm, then chest, and moved its beaked self toward his neck. Jack saw the chaos and kicked over to help his friend.

Now any scuba diver with any naturalism experience will know that the octopus' archenemy is the eel, and in Baja the green eel in particular. The two green eels in pursuit of the photographer caught sight of the octopus around Freddy's neck. They changed flight plans and bore down on Freddy.

The octopus too realized that something was amiss. His sharp eyes caught sight of the eels with their jaws agape. The octopus did the only sensible thing he could do and ejected silky black ink into the water. The confounded eels scuttled by the divers in two different directions. The contours of a nearby rock shifted mysteriously.

Pepe exhaled. He signaled hastily for the divers to converge and follow him. The pilots and photographer heeled Pepe obediently. Casually, Pepe swam toward an outcrop on the seamount.

A fluffy bed of cherry-red sea anemones anchored on the spent mass of lava. Their pink jelly arms swayed in the current. Sticky tips on their limbs indiscriminately groped the water searching for plankton. As the divers' fingers fell on the anemones' arms they instantly constricted back into their bodies.

The anemones glistened as Pepe swept his hand across them. It was as if he was stroking the flames of an intense fire. The photographer jockeyed next to Pepe and fired his strobe repeatedly. The sharp bursts of light forever froze the delicate beauty of the anemones.

Gus swam behind the other divers, enjoying their fascination with the anemones. He marveled at the splendor around him, the diving was raw and uncomplicated. Equipment and a boat, that was all one needed. The seamount placed a grain of sand in his heart that dive. Each rubber fin kick dissipated thoughts of his world and this grain of sand became his pearl.

Pepe corralled the divers. They had spent forty-five minutes in the water and their tanks were low enough to surface. He motioned upwards and the divers inflated their vests. The group rose awkwardly, like the wax in a lava lamp. Pepe signaled Jack and Fred to slow their ascents. The photographer was still on the sea floor finishing his roll of film. Gus and Meghan rose slowly from the bottom.

The group surfaced from the dive to a gentle breeze. The sky was big and blue and Sea Zephyr napped serenely in the distance. They back-floated. Pepe took his spare regulator and inflated the long orange buoy that looked like a sausage waving on the water's surface. Almost immediately, rumbling engine noises filled the divers' ears. Gentle waves that had come up during lunch had been blown away and were again replaced with a smooth surface. The divers formed a human ribbon while Sea Zephyr motored over to them.

Javier grabbed each diving rig and set it up on Sea Zephyr. He snapped elastic ties over the valves and anchored the tanks to the boat. In his nimble hands seven systems were aboard in minutes. Javier's competence gave the divers the distinct impression that they were with the best boat captain in the world. They probably were, his niche ability to charm time into slowing made the divers' vacation last longer than seemed possible.

After leaving the water the divers peeled their wetsuits down to their hips and left them like that. The fresh air felt good on their skin. Droplets rolled down their backs forming thin veins of crystallized salt on their shoulders and backs.

The afternoon sun soon sat uncomfortably hot on their skin. It burned rather than dried; summer here was not tranquil, but rather a burning bath of lava seemingly splashed upon one's body. It pulsed red and freckled the darkest skin. Loose cotton clothes hurriedly appeared from backpacks and draped the divers like the Mexican aristocracy they felt they were.

Pepe boarded the boat last. He pulled in the tow line with taunt forearm muscles developed with repeated natural work. The ladder swung up as the last of the tow line was reeled in. Javier took the clanging of the ladder as a signal to fire up the engines. They burned loud and flat; a low roar controlled by the sea water. Pepe crab-walked to the bow and raised the anchor.

The nylon slipped up easily and fell quickly into a daisy chain while the last ten feet of chain clanged with each link against the fiberglass boat. Pepe stowed the anchor in the pit on the boat, flipped the hatch closed, and muscled Javier away from the wheel. The divers secured any lose items and then were off.

Sea mist enveloped the boat. Loose hair tumbled and took to the wind. Pepe found the trip back from a dive to be a reflective time for most people. The divers sat together now talking like lifelong friends. Pepe smiled knowingly, the sea brought people together.

For a long while they simply pushed ahead skipping along on the sea like a flat rock. But soon something caught Pepe's eye. The transparent sunning surface water ahead was telling. Pepe instinctively followed the sea and saw a pod of dolphins pursuing something. The rubbery mammals were using a dive and surface pattern. Pepe swung Sea Zephyr toward the action and asked Javier in Spanish to get out the bucket.

"The bucket" was in fact a slated milk crate that had other uses besides storing the lead weight for the dive belts. Pepe veered closer and the dolphins dove. The photographer spun up another roll of film. There was nothing in the water. The boat was silent. Suddenly a fat, wide school of purple squid surfaced!

Javier leaned over Sea Zephyr and scooped them with the milk crate. He crated one load of squid after another. It was tough work and by the time "the bucket" got back on the boat only a handful of the squid had actually stayed inside it. This rudimentary method, however, soon had a score of squid flapping and squirting black ink everywhere; in the air, on the scuba gear, and at mesmerized divers.

"Let me try!" Gus slid over and relieved Javier.

It was hard work because the seawater was heavy. Gus lasted just five scoops until he was almost pulled over the side of the boat into the water. Jack saved him and took the crate as recourse, then Pepe was at it. Laughing tears dribbled down his checks. Jack pulled out a bunch more then his arms fell limp as well. They were all having a time of it until the pilot-less Sea Zephyr veered too sharply into its own wake and threw Meghan over the side. A curt scream ended their squid challenge. Pepe jumped back over to the wheel and picked up the young bride.

"Going in right after them Meghan?" Lisa smiled over to her as Gus helped Meghan out of the water. Gus just shook his head laughing. He realized that they had all taken a step back in time. It was a free land here where your hair could still float in the breeze, where a man could still be judged on his prowess with a slated basket, and where a young woman's laughter meant something.

Gus listened to the noise of life around him as the other divers talked about the day's events. They all seemed so content with life in this exact instant, but would it last? The seamount had done something to all of them; of that he was certain. Gus leaned back against his chair and looked towards the front of the boat. Pepe looked back at him and their eyes connected.

# CHAPTER 21

The sun came off its perch and rolled lower. By four o'clock the store windows creaked open again and siesta's slumber awoke. Women clothed themselves and men drank lemonade so bitter it sweetened thoughts of their work to come. Across the bay fishing boats rejoined the familiarity of shore. They appeared singularly, then in handfuls. These were the very boats that ventured daily past sight of land into the Sea of Cortez and often found themselves in opportunistic straits between the peninsula and mainland. One knew what lay on either side; the mainland offered the fisherman a larger market, but even as they approached the continent the water got a little darker and the clouds seemed to hover a little lower. The peninsula offered a fraction of the market, and lower prices at that, but the clouds held higher here and the ominous discontent that perpetually hovered above the mainland didn't exist on the peninsula. So the boats went far and wide for the day, yet always remained tethered to their true home.

Mari began to work the second shift. Typically the hours following siesta were the dullest with the tourists shopping the stores to which workers returned. She carted in another crate of mixed fruit that included kiwis, bananas, peaches, oranges, pears, and apples. She drew out her cutting board again and the shiny fillet knife she used to slice fruit.

The shop door swung open and her lanky helper arrived from school. Orlando came in on most summer afternoons to work at the ice cream store. He was still wearing the dark pants, white shirt, and tie characteristic of almost every Mexican school uniform. Orlando was ten now and acted more responsible than his twenty year-old peers. He instinctively went into the back room and changed into his working clothes, which consisted of an old, but clean pair of jeans, a collared shirt, and a crisp white apron his mother ironed to perfection. Orlando removed several trays of ice, a bag of salt, and brought them to the ice cream machines. He went back to get a second bag of salt.

Mari carried out two large jugs of cream, shook them for a moment, and tested the freshness with a lingering smell.

The churning of ice cream machines began in earnest for the evening customers.

# CHAPTER 22

Sea Zephyr zipped along the wave crests. The landscape overtook the intermittent conversation and the divers lulled into imaginative trances. They were all burned to some degree, even with the cotton clothing, heavy American sunscreen, and wide-rimmed hats. It didn't matter, this was Mexico in the summer.

Their mouths were parched. The warm air seemed to evaporate the very moisture from their skin. Only the Mexicans, it seemed, could endure the heat and diving combination. The rest were enveloped in a sleepy cloud. Their eyes gazed along the flat, steaming horizon with a longing look of anticipation for a lapse in the beating of the sun's rays. Even the flocking birds so common this morning found themselves baiting the water in an afternoon siesta.

Pepe steered the bow around the algae-encrusted green buoy and idled the engines. They choked for an instant, coughed, then steadied themselves. Sea Zephyr made her way into the outskirts of the harbor. On their left was the large PEMEX plant. A perpetual thin film of oil ran off into the bay from an uncapped discharge pipe and collated on the surface. Pepe glared at the plant.

The boat and plant passed each other slowly, knowingly. The plant had grown on this land like a barnacle and extended its tenacious grip onto neighboring cattle land, then reached further to the road system pausing to connect itself with the ferry barge that brought trailers from the mainland. The gray steel shell had "PEMEX" painted on it in caustic green.

Pepe looked back at the divers and then another glance more to his engines running the gasoline. He needed the plant, though, and he knew it. It was the Mexicans themselves who had embraced the sweeping change of the diesel engine and gasoline vehicles. Their electricity, their water pumps, their very way of life now seemed undeniably tied to PEMEX's existence.

# CHAPTER 23

Cervantes had long been established as a card cheat, both to himself and people with whom he played. Hence it came as no surprise when he was banished again from the daily card game at the wharf. It was more of a ritual than a branding. The onset of his cheating was unusual in the sense that he didn't cheat unless he was winning anyway, then when it came time for him to collect the pot he would carelessly drop an extra card from his palm.

Undeterred, he walked back now to the shop. He had passed this stretch of La Paz for many years now and had acquaintances on both sides of the street. They were always eager to learn of his fortunes for the day or what pottery he was working on next. Cervantes took a plastic bag from his pocket and removed two sour gummy candies. He had become addicted to these digestive nightmares.

Cervantes haggered down the boulevard stopping to peek inside his neïghbors' shop windows. He procrastinated to the last, finally though he did come to his shop. A bunch of letters had found their way into his mailbox again. Cervantes grabbed the lot and opened his door.

The kiln had grown quiet after pulling the teacups from the heat. There still was an essence of juniper in the air. Drawn out, fired, and painted beautifully the teacups were now on the window shelf cooling. The glaze he used had reacted well with the paint giving his cups a shimmering glint.

Cervantes picked up one of the teacups and held it in the light. It sparkled. Cervantes knew the tea Mr. Vasquez would drink from these cups would be exquisite, but would the cups give their tea away so willingly?

"Hello?" The telephone ringing stopped.

"Yes, Cervantes, this is Mr. Vasquez. I was wondering the status of my teacups. Have you finished them?" He asked his questions like statements.

"Yes, yes señor, they are complete. They were fired this afternoon and I have just come back from playing cards now." The last part of the sentence got away from Cervantes and he immediately felt ashamed for letting it slide so casually to Mr. Vasquez that he had been gambling. Apparently more than a tinge of his previous employer's clout still remained programmed in him.

Mr. Vasquez was disgruntled to know that Cervantes hadn't been watching the teacups for the entire time and let his intonation reflect his displeasure. "Well I must, just must, have them by tomorrow evening. Will it be possible for you to bring them over to the PEMEX plant for me? We will be having an afternoon tea and I want to use my teacups."

"Yes, yes señor, I will bring them over personally tomorrow afternoon. I must still let them cool now and put the finishing touches on for you but they will be ready by tomorrow evening." Cervantes let the conditioned, and comfortable, response flow from his lips.

"Very well, Cervantes. I will see you tomorrow." Mr. Vasquez ended the telephone conversation without the courtesy of an adios.

Cervantes put the worn receiver back on the wall. He walked on the creaking pine planks over to where he had fired the teacups. All twelve sat there beautifully, several of them already had taken on a life of their own. Cervantes took a damp cloth and rubbed the cups down with small dabs of extra virgin olive oil. He brought their finish up to snuff and admired his work. The paint was magnificent and glistened just like Esperenza's skin. Each polished mango cup was placed near the window to ripen up in the last rays of the day's sun.

Steady feet moved over to a desk anchored to the floor. Cervantes opened his diary. He wrote how he was caught cheating at cards when a couple walked into his boat. They were young and frisky Americans who, to all appearances, were looking for some pottery to take home with them.

"Buenos Dias, how can I help you on this lovely day?" Cervantes the salesman came to life.

"Lovely indeed, lovely indeed," the man in an unequivocally English accent replied. "Look here dear, he has quite a collection of drawing bowls that you should fancy." The English fellow picked up a flowered bowl that had inclinations of the sun in various phases on the rim and a reflective blue undertone on the interior. He palmed the drawing bowl and examined it for economic consideration.

"No, no, Steward that is far too brisk for our taste." She squirmed past him to where her eyes could follow the contours of Baja Pottery. Her pupils dilated when she caught sight of the teacups drying on the window.

"What," in an exaggerated yet fully English accent "are those? They are simply beautiful, I must have them!" She zipped over to the window ledge and picked up one of the teacups. She held it like a child holding a crystal ball.

"Ah señora, I'm afraid they are already sold." Cervantes secretly smiled as he observed her fascination with his work. He knew the truest test of one's work was to have it sought from a distance with no advertising.

"My dear sir, but at what price? Surely you could make more and sell these to me?" Her eyelids fluttered.

"Señora, they are sold at a price I am not at liberty to discuss." Each word the tourist spoke heightened Cervantes' sense of accomplishment. He let his arms, then hands, fall gently behind his back and stood silently.

"And to whom, may I ask, did you sell these drops of heaven to?" Her words became sweeter as her intent grew.

"You may inquire to Mr. Vasquez, the PEMEX Baja president, of his desire to part with these heirlooms."

She was neither pleased nor displeased with the answer she received, but at least content in knowing someone of some importance had commissioned such beautiful work. She eased her suffering, and increased her husband's, with the purchase of a drawing bowl and a cachet of pots. Nevertheless, she turned to give the teacups a farewell glance as she left the landlocked boat.

# CHAPTER 24

For the third and final time of the day, the salted nylon rope took to the air. It fell limply on the dock. Javier jumped off Sea Zephyr, picked up the rope, and wrapped it securely to the chrome post in one fell swoop.

The divers had the look of resignation upon their brow. The scuba diving, boat ride, and sun had conspired against them. They took their gear from the boat and put it on a dolly Javier brought from the ship. He lugged the vests, wet suits, weights, and tanks up to the dive shop. He plunged the lot into a big plastic bin filled with fresh water. Javier bathed the equipment in the water for several minutes and then let the gear dry on plastic racks above the shop's cement floor.

Pepe cut the engine. He grabbed the bucket of squid and with Jack's help raised it off the boat. They had retained their pink tone even in death and their eyes where dilated wide, wide open as if they could see the whole world around them at once. Jack and Freddy carted the bucket of squid over to the exterior of the dive shop where a ready made cutting board, hose, and fillet knife extended from the wall.

Lisa helped Pepe gather up the remaining dive gear and the divers, en masse, entered the dive shop. Pepe arranged a round of drinks.

The lemonades were cold and bitter. The divers drank thirstily and Pepe refilled their glasses a second time before a single cup ring had formed on the table.

"So how was it everyone?" Pepe's eyes scanned the divers for a response. Sitting down hydrated he knew he had the best chance of getting a reply. It had taken twenty minutes for the divers to leave the boat and settle into a thinking state of mind again; it appeared they were still at the fifteen minute mark.

Meghan reached the conversational point a little earlier than the rest "Well it was truly amazing, how's that for a canned answer?" She laughed the carefree laugh of a just married woman. "I mean the water was wonderfully warm and we saw so much life today."

The pilots had switched from lemonade to beer, along with Javier, and began to reflect on the finer points of life. In particular, each was thinking of the type of woman he'd like to be sleeping with tonight.

The camera was rewinding the last of the rolls of film. The photographer was pleased with the trip. He had taken five full rolls of film, one on each dive, another during lunch, and two more during the boat rides to and from the dive site. The photographer dried the plastic casing with a towel and unlatched the camera's cover.

The blue plastic o-ring was still snug around the shell of the inner camera to prevent leaking underwater. The o-ring itself was riding on a thin layer of silicon that kept the seal tight. The roll of film was neatly tucked in the belly of the camera. He removed it and put it in a black plastic canister and disassembled the camera on the wood counter as they talked about the diving.

Having acted as the conversation catalyst, Pepe now just leaned back and let the divers talk. This is what he longed for in life, to hear them after diving the seamount. It was his theory that one of three things happened after diving the seamount; the most common being a diver simply filed it away as a satisfying memory. Occasionally a diver's current lifestyle was reinforced; he could see this in Lisa every time she dove here with them. The most special, and the one he particularly always kept an eye out for, was the awakening.

"No, it was more than that honey," Gus looked at his wife and at the group. "Don't you all feel it?"

"Feel what?" laughed Javier.

"The energy around that place?"

"Dude, you need to have a beer!" Jack pushed Gus a bottle he had just popped open. Freddy raised his glass in the air and toasted.

"To Pepe and Javier, and all of Mexico, for a wonderful, okay Gus, 'energetic" day of diving!" Freddy tipped the bottle back and let the beer stream down his throat.

"What do you mean by 'energy' Gus?" The photographer was still fidgeting with the camera on the table, but the conversation caught his attention.

Gus let the photographer's question distill the air. His mind refined the words coming to his mouth. And drip by drip Gus spoke softly, like any worthwhile meditation, "The seamount's energy and power just seemed to come upon me fully."

Pepe looked at, then through Gus, towards the seamount. His heart skipped a beat and he sighed softly to himself. Pepe lowered his head and contemplated what the group's reaction would be.

The photographer nodded his head in agreement. "I mean I did see a lot of great animals and a terrific landscape here, so if you mean those things then I guess you're right, there is a lot of energy in the landscape."

Meghan looked over to her husband as he took a sip of the beer. Gus nodded in agreement with the photographer then paused for a moment. Lisa was smiling at him.

"Gus," Lisa reached over and grabbed a beer Jack had slid her way, "you seemed to have discovered the magic, the energy you call it, of this place. It's definitely here, I feel it too. I mean that's why I decided to move down here."

Pepe licked his lips. He smiled to himself and let them lead the conversation as he stood up and walked into the dive shop. Pepe grabbed a plate and piled it high with tortilla chips. A bowl of fresh salsa was in the refrigerator. He took that over to the table and let the divers share the chips and salsa.

Pepe walked to the filet table and cleaned the squid within earshot of the conversation unfolding around him.

"One day you just decided to move here?" Jack looked over to Lisa incredulously.

"Yeah, I sure did." She smiled back at him. She enjoyed him putting his eyes on her. Lisa knew that the attraction he had of her wasn't physical, but rather an admiration of her lifestyle. "I came here gradually at first in my mind, but the magic I found finally overtook me. I had to live here—it was what felt right for me."

"So what'd you do?" Freddy was warming up to the conversation and the rest of the group listened intently, for a person must do something.

"Does it really matter?" Lisa played along.

Freddy thought for a moment. "Well, no it really doesn't matter what you do, so long as you do something. Something that'll pay to live."

"Hmmm...that's an interesting concept." Lisa smiled and looked over at Pepe filleting the squid. She knew he could hear everything but he made no indication of it. Lisa let her fingers fall to her knee and rubbed the scar nervously. She wondered if this group was ready for a serious conversation.

"Ah, this is nonsense Lisa," Javier jumped in. "I mean you need to work at something, this life isn't free. We have to fight for what we have here, you of all people should know that."

"But look at the wonderful place in which you live!" Meghan stretched her arms high into the air and yawned. She swept her arm around the dive shop and across the bay and landed it squarely around Gus's neck.

"A wonderful place you say? Yes, but this is a small town and we don't have all the things a big city does." Javier dipped his chip into the salsa and crunched down on it.

"I believe you're both right, but my question still goes back to this energy around the seamount." Gus cleaned his throat and continued. "And taking that feeling to the next level, I'd just like to throw this out on the table, which I think we're all talking about anyway. It's a question of freedom, and what it's worth to you?"

"OK Gus, and what's the meaning of life? Ha!" Jack slapped his knee.

"Well, since you brought it up, what's it to you Jack?" Gus grinned back.

Pepe put down the filleting knife and listened intently. The pure question had been raised. Would they continue down this path of discovery or would they turn their heads like so many others before them had? Pepe grabbed the excess cuttings, the excuses, and tossed them into the water. A hungry swarm of bait fish enveloped the chum and make quick work of it. Pepe brought the fillets into the kitchen at the back of the dive shop. He went around front and took a bowl of batter from the refrigerator.

The photographer finished cleaning and disassembling his camera and now fully rejoined the group's conversation.

"So the question on the table," Javier made himself the moderator, "is what is freedom?"

"It's a lot of things to a lot of different people. For some it might be money, for others the ability to move without a wheelchair, for others it might be escaping from prison. That's a really broad topic honey!" Meghan smiled over at Gus. Her hair draped along her shoulder blades and her metallic sunglasses reflected his image.

"No, no I agree sweetie. It is a broad topic, but ultimately isn't freedom always independence?" Gus laid his cards on the table.

"Or is it a lack of dependence?" Lisa edged in. She had let the comment slip in the conversation as thin and strong as a stiletto. Its curtness, she was sure, would quickly offend. But the fuse was lit.

"Where the hell did you get that one Lisa?" Jack laughed loudly as his beer-shot eyes rolled. "That's BS, freedom is doing what you want, whenever you want."

"Do you think you have that?" She retorted.

"Of course not, no one does. We just work and work, and occasionally take a vacation to give us a break. That's when we're really free, or at least for a little bit." The beer emptied in Jack's mouth. His hand instinctively reached for another.

"No," the photographer started, always choosing a decisive moment to interject. "Freedom is a matter of opportunity cost."

"Opportunity cost?" Javier looked up from the travel magazine that had taken over his interest.

"Definitely," replied the photographer.

Lisa smiled at the young man who seemed to know so much, so soon. Pepe came to the table with a sombrero-sized plate of sizzling fried squid. They looked delectable. He placed the hot plate on the worm wood table. He cut up a couple limes in his hand using a pocket knife and spread the slices on the calamari plate. Pepe motioned over to Javier. Javier reached below the table and pulled out a stack of small plates, took one for himself first, and passed the rest around the table.

"So, where has the conversation gone to now?" Pepe inquired with a hint of sarcasm that suspected they had drifted into folly.

"We have, or I should say the photographer here has, brought in the idea that 'freedom is opportunity cost.'" Javier summed up the situation.

Pepe's face softened. His hands were weathered and his face toned by days spent outside working a man's life, but his heart was fresh. And it skipped a beat.

"Opportunity cost you say?" Pepe's lips mouthed the words his chest breathed. He exhaled his breath like it was his last. "Opportunity cost…hmmm…yes, the choice not to live, but to take a life given to you. Opportunity cost and time, they hold each other's hand in our lifetime." Pepe finished his words with a look towards Gus.

"Ahh…yes, the classic formula for Hollywood success," Freddy's eyes were lit by the setting sun, "'carpe diem' and 'be yourself.' With those two things at your back a person will never fail." Calamari crackled in Freddy's mouth. He chased down the squid with beer.

"Americans," Javier's bitter thoughts became words "with your 'carpe diem' and 'being yourself' make it sound like a spiritual journey you all have to take along with the SUV, dog, and two kids...in Mexico we do not have that privilege..."

Pepe murmured "or burden."

Gus looked over at Javier. He understood where he was coming from. "You simply work and try to enjoy the life provided. Those of you successful enough can do this all your lives, but the rich start to imitate Americans and become miserable."

"I don't know," Javier's eyes glistened, "the American lifestyle looks pretty good to me. What's not to like? Beautiful women, fast cars, everything so new!" Javier's eyes glistened.

"I second that!" Jack tipped his bottle toward Javier.

"And I third it!" Freddy attempted to tip his bottle, but dropped it instead.

# Chapter 25

The baking summer sun would keep the homes warm until early morning even as it dipped below the horizon and left a thin veil of orange skirting the horizon. This is when La Paz truly started getting its second wind, since the first hours after siesta were spent recovering from siesta. But when the sun fell, that signaled the change from siesta to fiesta. The shops filled with the dust from swinging doors. Young men who had the sense to work, and there were many of them, were on the steps of the family businesses sweeping the sidewalk.

Mari loved this part of the day, people were most apt to come in and sit and talk about things. It was when the tourists always came back and the ice cream melted down their hands. They would lick their hands and continue their conversations as though everything in the world was fine. And it was. She saw contentment in their eyes.

An American couple, she could always tell by the fashion of their clothes, walked through the doors. He had a strong face, wrinkled in just the right places with the frequency of a smile. She came a little past his shoulder and wore her blond hair tied back in a pony tail. Their clothes were of the light cotton travel type. Mari had fashioned herself to be wearing those someday as she strolled through some foreign city or another.

He came up to the glass counter and looked at Mari's handiwork. The ice creams, the second batch, had been done for nearly an hour now. The smell of cream and cut fruit still filled the room.

"Mmmm...yes, that ginger peach ice cream looks absolutely wonderful! Could I have a scoop of that?" He motioned over to the container. "Honey, what do you think?"

"So many choices Gus!" Meghan reached for his outstretched hand and nestled next to him on the glass counter. Her deep green eyes scanned the selection, hesitating on the cherry. "I want that one, the cherry!" Her eyes followed Mari's hand as she scooped a cone of cherry ice cream.

"There you are, that will be fifty pesos," Mari handed Gus his ginger peach ice cream. Her hand grazed against his and for an instant he could feel all of her life in him. The softness, the color, and the passion all enveloped him. Gus blinked at her.

"Sweety, you do have fifty pesos?" Meghan smiled at him.

"Oh, of course I'm sorry!" Gus reached into his blue jean pocket and took out three twenties and gave them to the girl. "Thank you that will be quite all right."

Gus smiled at her and led his wife to the terrace. It was becoming a beautiful night to eat ice cream. The stars were already up.

Pepe too had just gotten home in the city. His day was over, but in many ways it was just beginning. He thanked Javier for the ride and rapped the truck with his hand. His door opened and Esperenza stood at the threshold looking him over.

"Well, how was it today?" She asked him this everyday and he always answered the same, that it was wonderful to dive for a living. A dinner of green chile chicken enchiladas waited in the oven. Pepe took the bottle of Tequila behind the cabinet and poured himself and Esperenza short orders. He didn't touch his drink, but rather stepped around the table toward the bathroom.

He peeled off his clothing and wiped himself down with a hot towel. He dipped the towel in a soapy bath and exaggerated the strokes on his cheek he knew Esperenza was watching to imply his work day was harder than it really was.

"You old donkey, come in here when you're done. We must eat!" She giggled at his ever-changing antics.

Pepe put on fresh clothes and walked out to the garden. The moon had risen. It gave the cacti long, broad shadows. Pepe let the night into his body and breathed a deep breath. He let it fill his lungs and exhaled it slowly to let the full weight of his body calm with the passing of his breath. It was starry and light but not overly quiet. Even now the sounds from the city rose above the tiled roofs and into the night.

"Are you enjoying the night?" Esperenza's eyes filled his as she drew on his clothes and brought his body close to hers. Pepe brushed her hair with his fingertips and parted her lips with his. The night air warmed and the food stayed in the oven for some time.

# CHAPTER 26

Lisa drove her white Landcruiser, to which she had affixed "Todo Santos Landscaping" in forest green, to the front of the hotel. She picked up the photographer and the two pilots as they had made arrangements to meet up for dinner downtown.

Jack and Freddy were still a bit dehydrated and woozy, i.e. drunk, to be driving so they split the back seat between themselves and their egos. The photographer joined Lisa in the front and they started out. The road into town was narrow and sharp but was quickly replaced with a wider boulevard when they came into La Paz proper. The city was buzzing with activity as the latent effects of the sun cooled and the sound of music filled the air.

They drove along the main drag looking for a place to park. Lisa slowed at the speed bump, lest she risk damaging the elevated undercarriage. The speed bumps, "topes," in Mexico tended to be Jersey barrier equivalents in the United States. Her wheels peaked over the tope and they saw Gus and Meghan crossing the street towards the harbor. Lisa waved and shouted out. Gus flipped back around and gave a thumbs up. He motioned down the street to a restaurant that was perched over the water. Lisa pulled the Landcruiser over to a street spot and the crew filed out into the restaurant.

# CHAPTER 27

Javier knew he had to raise the stakes in the game. Already Cervantes was onto his plan and he knew any further lapse in time could cost him the girl. He had talked with Pepe on the ride home and couldn't come up with better ideas on how to seduce the woman. He cased Fresh Fruit Ice Cream until it became seemingly impossible not to enter so he walked in and proceeded over to the counter.

His palms were sweaty before a word fell from his lips. He just looked at her. He didn't know quite what to say. He hated these moments of indecision. She was wearing her beautiful cooking apron again, the one with all the stains smudged in from cutting fruit. He thought of what crafty words to say to her. She turned around towards him, then it was too late. She had turned like a top on him.

"Oh, Buenos Noches Javier," Mari smiled sweetly at him. It was the simple smile of a woman that turns a man into a pile of flubbering jelly. He knew it was a mistake to have come tonight. His chubby cheeks flushed.

"Buenos Noches Mari." He mouthed the words back and never considered speaking until he had spoken. They were alone in Fresh Fruit Ice Cream and Javier knew he had just exercised all of his vocabulary.

"So did you go out scuba diving today?" Mari stepped around the counter and positioned herself in front of the Fresh Fruit Ice Cream counter. Her arms crossed her chest as she leaned back against the counter. She flushed full.

"Yes," Javier happily thought to himself that this was a topic he was well versed and seemingly competent in, "we went to the seamount today for two dives with a group of Americans."

"Oh yes, what type of Americans?" Why did her eyes light up when she said that? Javier grimaced. He knew he had said too much already. Now of course she would want to hear about what these Americans did.

"Well just the regular sort I guess." Would that work he wondered?

"Yes of course, but what did they do?" Obviously it wasn't enough he knew now.

He started to explain. "We had two pilots and a professional couple that…"

"Yes, I must have met them before you came in, a nice pair those two." She smiled wryly at Javier and edged forward. "Javier, how come you have never asked me to go diving at the seamount?"

"Well good evening my princess!" Cervantes came in the room with a large parcel. Cervantes brushed by Javier until he realized it was Javier and then he made a purposeful effort to seem dismayed.

Javier feigned happiness to see Cervantes. He nodded respectfully when Cervantes brought Mari into his arms and gave her a sweeping hug.

Javier's insides trembled for a moment then relaxed as a group of school children bustled into the store. It was as if all of his soul had just been squeezed out by this man. Had Mari really just asked him why he had never taken her to dive the seamount? Had he been ignorant of her feelings for him all this time?

"Children, children!" Cervantes gruffed "Be careful of that package if you know what's good for you." Cervantes let his voice fall again as the children stepped away from the parcel. Javier looked down and noticed that it was made out to his father.

Javier moved towards the box to pick it up when he heard Cervantes rumble, "I thank you for your obvious request to deliver that package to your father but I cannot allow it for I always personally deliver my product."

Especially, Javier thought, if there was a tip in it for him. The sense of unwelcome peaked, Javier nodded and made his way towards the door. He looked back to see if Mari followed his eyes, but she didn't. There was a ridiculously long line of children pressing toward her. Javier had let his head sink only to have it placed back on the clouds when she tossed him a wink on his last step out. Javier let the mesh door fall behind him and shudder on the frame. Javier's step was deliberate now, for a man that believes he has the heart of the girl he loves is sure.

Javier walked along the main drag for fifteen minutes, passing his truck along the way. He lit a cigarette, looked at it full in his eyes then snubbed it out. Yes, he thought, that's the girl for me. And for the first time in a very long time felt like he had made some progress. Javier gazed into the sky towards the stepped hills;

then for the next several hours he debated to himself if that actually was a wink or something in her eye.

# CHAPTER 28

Gus watched the blue sea fall beneath the plane's wings. They rose higher and higher into the air. The plane pitched to the right and headed north towards Los Angeles. It flew along the coast for the length of a goodbye and then reached a higher altitude. He thumbed his wedding ring and thought what it would be like to escape the rat race. To leave, to live, he wondered. His hand stroked Meghan's hair. A sigh escaped his lips and the pearl grew larger.

# CHAPTER 29

Cervantes, although he worked in a boat docked permanently on land, was not one for boats. This surprised even him as it was natural for all people, especially Baja Mexicans perceivably, to be both amiable and proficient in the sea. Cervantes was neither.

He was particularly slow getting on the dingy which was to take him to the PEMEX plant. He had packed the cups tightly in a wood case to avoid damaging the fine pieces in transit. Each cup was singularly wrapped in tissue paper then wedged snuggly into the partitioned section of the wood case.

The boat motored along and exhausted a cloud of diesel. Cervantes relaxed and placed the teacups on the edge of the boat to lessen the burden on his knees, knees worn creaky from spending hours crouched in tight spots welding PEMEX distribution lines. The work had taken a heavy physical toll on him.

More menial than ever meaningful, day after day of working in fumed environments unfit for most any life had drained Cervantes. Welding without always wearing eye protection had caused his eyes to be very sensitive to the sun. He squinted often now and big-footed crow's feet nested on the corners of his eyes. He watched the waves ahead suspiciously.

They bounced along in the dinghy for ten, then fully twenty minutes. Finally, it seemed so long to him, Cervantes saw the concrete PEMEX steps coming up from the water in the distance. Overwhelming its foundation, the PEMEX plant stood fully flexed in front of him. Thick piping wound around the compound while heavy gauge steel fence topped nicely with razor wire protected the plant.

Puffs of dark smoke escaped the tall stacks at regular intervals and plumed into the sky.

The water ferry sputtered to a stop and Cervantes lifted his stiff legs off the boat straddling the dock. He raised his foot and stepped onto dry land. All too fast, though, his other foot caught the boat's edge. He stumbled backward. The crate dropped from his hands. Cervantes' eyed flashed just once as the teacups hit the edge of the concrete stairs. The case shattered and teacups dashed into the air, smashed on the concrete, and two fell into the ocean. They loitered on the surface for a moment, sipped the water, then dove.

Cervantes screamed. He was beside himself cursing aloud. Shattered cup pieces on the stairs were still spinning. Three others were marred, and two were now on the bottom of the ocean. The tea was to be in less than an hour and now only six undamaged teacups remained. Cervantes gathered the three marred teacups together and put the shards into the boat. He scrambled around and sized up the remaining six that had stayed protected in the bottom of the wooden crate.

Mr. Vasquez saw all of the commotion from his balcony and rushed down the stairs to see what Cervantes had done. He shuffled past his executive secretary who was lost in thought deciding what to have for dinner this evening while simultaneously contemplating the merits of getting a shorter haircut. Vasquez came upon Cervantes. His moustache sizzled when he saw his teacups grouped up in Cervantes arms.

"What is the meaning of this?" Vasquez' eyes flared.

"Ahh...Mr. Vasquez, I am so sorry señor. So sorry. My foot slipped as I was getting of the boat. I dropped the wooden crate."

"Well, are any of my teacups damaged?" Vasquez mentally began counting the teacups in Cervantes arms.

Cervantes read the account slowly as the scene played itself over again in his mind. "Yes señor, one is completely shattered, three severely damaged, and two are lost at sea."

"Lost at sea?" A question mark arose on Vasquez' brow.

"They tumbled over the dock and into the water when I dropped the package," Cervantes confessed as he motioned to the water's edge.

"Well, you shall have no payment for these teacups then."

Cervantes moaned aloud and shook his head. "Señor please, I have six beautiful teacups for you."

Mr. Vasquez looked at the cups Cervantes was now cradling in his arms. They were indeed beautiful. The coloring was magnificent and the design perfectly executed. They had a certain life to them. Maybe he wanted these after all.

"Well, I shall only pay a quarter of the price as they come to me in such a state. And consider yourself lucky I pay you even that." Vasquez threw out his bait.

Cervantes nodded silently. Mr. Vasquez removed two bills from his wallet and gave them to Cervantes. Vasquez motioned him to be on his way. Cervantes said nothing to the boatman the entire trip back home. An air of gloom filled his big heart. He contemplated nothing but his loss, then he remembered fondly that he still had three teacups, albeit damaged, here for himself! While not altogether in the best shape they were still quite exquisite, and of his own belief, his finest work yet. He stopped near the dock on the way to his home to play cards.

# CHAPTER 30

Mr. Vasquez hurriedly prepared for the tea. Senior guests from across Mexico were coming shortly to have a long-awaited tea with him. They were amongst the most influential, wealthy, and tyrannical men in the country. Mr. Vasquez looked again at the commissioned teacups and noted quite happily to himself the fantastic deal he had just gotten.

It was of no matter to him that a deal was small or large, but the thrill of him gaining some edge, or keeping the appearance of a superior position that mattered most to him. He was fiercely loyal to himself and let his staff know it. But perhaps more than himself, he was loyal to the guard; that old guard of Mexican individuals and families that had grown to control every facet of large corporations and government institutions.

He thought of it as one big family with many brothers and sisters. Mr. Vasquez felt himself a privileged, if not often overlooked, son in this family. He was head of the PEMEX Baja division, and his son Javier, when he finally came of age, would also be wrung up the ladder of established society.

The guests' cars started arriving. They were cordially shown into the sitting room Mr. Vasquez had prepared. A dozen of these men came today, men he referred to as the regales; regales in the sense that their riches, power, and influence made them a modern day plutocracy.

Small talk preceded large talk and presently each of the teacups executed in a traditional design by weary hands had the lips of a Mexican mogul on it. They drank scented tea full of flavor, sprinkled with a dash of milk, and feathered with fine sugar.

The cups kept the warm tea secure, but of design were wholly open to the advances of the moguls' lips. So the men sat, and occasionally stood, around the table and talked. Their thoughts, as their actions, were grand to both themselves and to those they could affect. They collectively controlled oil, farming, banking, government contracts, and a variety of mineral deposits. A few had the ears, some the throats, of politicians throughout the country. They cupped the teacups in their hands and swallowed the life from them with pleasure. It was their nature to feed off others so they drank deeply of this life.

Mr. Vasquez lifted his cup high in the air and proposed a toast. "To us," he began, "it is said belongs the spoils. We control the oil, food distribution, and even the very political make-up of the country." His words trailed off as the regales eyes gleamed with each passing word.

They had woven their web wide and its strands were strong. It was a net providing a great deal of comfort but at a price; an individual's liberty was sold for conveniences, life was effectively marginalized for the sake of creature comfort. The higher sense of enabling freedom was lost along the way. It was replaced by membership in this group of regales who made their life's pleasure indulging on the populace's toil. And the populace trudged on. It worked and worked at pulling from the ground. It mortgaged and debted, for wasn't that the way? It was inescapable to live any other way.

Freedom had grown distasteful and even callous in the minds of many. It was unacceptable to live one's life with a passion for being free. And it was to this that the regales drank their tea and toasted themselves again.

Every day they grew more successful by mass marketing their prosperity, in their hearts they could only hope to duplicate their peers success in the United States; there 5% of the population controlled 90% of the wealth and the population was largely marginalized to watching television and occasionally delving into serialized book clubs for expanding their horizons.

The regales wanted to build on this impressive start. They had gathered today to push forward a revolutionary idea to lure a whole generation of Americans to Mexico; the casino-hospital. Hoards of geriatric Americans, if convinced, could live their lives medicated and gambling. It didn't seem too hard a sell.

# CHAPTER 31

More and more Gus sought peace, if not solace in his life. This conclusion was based on a growing knowledge that it was much easier to get into something than it was to get out of it. Proportionally, if it was extremely difficult to get into something, it was nearly impossible to get out of it.

Gus leaned back in his plush chair and looked around his office. It was cold. He rolled his chair back, stood up, and moved over to the window. He looked out on to the city. Snow was falling and had made great gains against the battalion of ploughs combating it. It was incessant. His gaze remained unbroken for some time. Gus turned and looked around his office again. His computer hummed on his desk. He realized he must have dozed off for a moment.

Gus was preparing an article for a law review and had been at it now for the better part of six hours. His desk was long and cherry and matched nicely with both the artwork adorning his walls and other pieces of furniture in the room. He looked around again for what he wanted to see but didn't see it. He wondered to himself whether he was suffering from just a particularly intense desire to leave the firm again or if this time it was something more.

He had grown restless. It was the restlessness of a man who wanted to live outside the world in which he felt trapped. His two year marriage with Meghan had been suffering. They had grown apart from their initial love and now had reached that most dangerous of places in a relationship, the status quo. Each pursued individual careers at the expense of their relationship. Their salaries reflected their professional dedication, but a growing emptiness in their lives was apparent.

Gus thought at first that it might be children, and that having a son or daughter would make life seem more fulfilling and exciting. But that wasn't it. And he knew it definitely wasn't the pursuit of more accolades from work or the purchase of a new home. No, it was something more than that. It was an intrinsic feeling in his soul that he knew was dying. A burning sensation filled his heart. It became painful.

His wandering eyes settled on his degrees plastered on the wall. He had spent his young life striving for the best grades so he could attend the "gifted" classes in high school. He worked his heart out in high school so he could get into Harvard. Like every other freshman in Cambridge he sought to find his niche and exploit that. He succeeded even more. He won a semester scholarship in London to pursue an economic thesis challenging the very nature of free market purchasing.

Upon his return he decided that law was his calling. He took weekend LSAT preparation classes and scored in the top 1% of his class, just like everyone else he knew. For three more years he attended school in Cambridge, with a summer spent in Spain researching maritime law. He stayed in Boston, four years after finishing law school, and already had been named a partner at a mid-sized firm. He'd taken the Autobahn to success, but looking back on his life it didn't look as successful as he originally thought.

Intellectually he had risen to the challenge and defeated opponents in his path, principally sloth and mediocrity. But there was something missing. In his pursuit of excellence he had overlooked the excellence of life. He sought more education, he yearned to learn but he had increasingly compartmentalized himself into himself. And he was not alone.

His friends had followed nearly identical tracks in their lives, perhaps not in the same field but, nonetheless in the same way. They had become medical specialists who focused solely on strands of DNA, scholars who looked only for clues in a field with only twenty researchers in the world, or business tycoons who drank their tea in the afternoon. He considered for a moment his life and all that he had. And naturally as people will often do when they consider what they have versus what they don't life suddenly seemed tolerable.

He mused to himself that he really didn't have anything to complain about. He had a beautiful wife, while not altogether in love with him, still tolerable. He owned a condominium and had enough money to live comfortably. He dined at nice restaurants and socialized with sharp minds. His counsel was respected, if not admired, and he was still so young. But again the burning fell upon him. The grain of sand burned and seared near his heart. He knew where it was and what caused him this pain. It was longing, longing for something he doubted he could have, for what everyone in his cynical world knew didn't exist.

It was scary and a subject that shouldn't be broached, either on a personal or professional sense. People talked. It wasn't healthy to have such ambitions or goals. Perhaps when he was old it became acceptable, but even then it was an acidic topic that begged careful consideration. The consequences would be dire. If freedom was so accessible and readily viable, well then, everyone would want it.

It was horrifying, working only when one wanted or doing what one loved? It was the adult equivalent of the most horrid childhood boogey tale. It was contrived simply to cause despair. One would be lonely doing it, for no more than a handful of super, super, super rich could do it. It was not for the common man. One had to work in the proletariat one belonged to; whether you sold hot dogs, were a secretary, made middle class wage, practiced medicine, or even owned your own profitable business. It didn't matter. Life was too short to enjoy. Better to work, be miserable, and take vacations that were frowned upon anyway. He too suffered greatly from that sadistic philosophy so prevalent in corporate America.

All these thoughts, he realized, had somehow over time been programmed into his head, and indeed his heart. Worse still, he let it happen. Gus smiled to himself and for the first time in all his life, he made plans for his escape.

# CHAPTER 32

They tumbled over the side of the boat into the water. The sky was clear and loosely dotted with clouds that made the underwater visibility super; the anchor line could be seen down to its perch on a head of rocks. Pepe kept his eyes on the gaggle of divers as they descended down on the seamount.

An experienced group of divers from Canada, they had flown in for a multi-day dive trip inspired by an article published two years ago by a photographer from Albuquerque, NM about the seamount. He published a two column feature in the downtown newspaper with several photos of the beautiful sea life. Apparently a Canadian travel editor had seen this piece and picked it up on his paper. Based on the article four friends got together and incorporated this dive foray into their annual winter migration south.

They fell from the water's surface like parachutists. Obviously this group of divers had dove together before. They were comfortable in the water and stabilized their descent gently. Pepe looked above as they dove down. The surface faded into a light, airy haze. A school of anchovies balled up and approached the divers curiously. They fanned wide and spread thin in their ranks. Their mouths gapped wide, then they closed, they swam faster and opened their mouths again. The school was filtering plankton from the rich water. The school tightened their ranks. A shadow in the distance spooked them. They formed a tight ball again. Instantly a sleek marlin darted into the center of the ball. It ripped its head back and forth.

The frenzied marlin turned, flipped, and spanked the school of anchovies. They dashed away, reconvened, then dashed away again as the marlin came at them.

Pepe followed the action above while tracking the divers below him. They were upon the seamount and investigating a crevice when suddenly a stone-colored grouper shot out towards them. He was excessively protective of the crevice and admonished the startled divers with a healthy dose of fright. He circled twice then swam away into the blue depths.

The divers kicked forward toward a soft flowering coral on the rocks. They took their time examining it. The coral was a heated orange color, even at this depth. Pepe pulled out his flashlight and shown it on the coral. With the added light the coral blazed. It crackled in pleasure with the addition paid to it and almost seemed to grimace as the divers passed over it toward a cluster of rock outcroppings in the distance. The little fireball faded back to a cooler orange and enjoyed the current kicked its way by the divers.

Pepe led them along the seamount's edge to a sheer wall where a tightly knit sea fan was anchored. It was the size of a basketball player's outstretched hands and had a frizzy wave pattern to its body. Pepe brought the divers in closer so they could see how the sea fan caught its dinner in the current. They dove over the seamount wall and fell to its level.

The water was noticeably cooler just several feet down. It was a current that ran along the seamount's waist. The fan waved softly as the dives kicked vigorously to maintain their position on the wall. They were unattached and taken forthright into the current. It was a strain to maintain the right level and buoyancy here, and Pepe only took these divers because of their comfort level in the water.

Pepe ascended and let his trunk sail away with the current to a higher ground. The group followed him up as he anchored himself with just two fingers on a rock ledge. He hung upside down and peered into the passage below. He lit up the cavern and the group looked in. They saw hundreds, if not thousands, of clear eggs draped from the ceiling in neat thin lines. The lines of eggs swayed in an unseen current coming from the mouth of the cavern. It was a warm, excessively warm, breeze of water that blew against the divers.

The water seemed thicker, richer with nutrients here. As the divers passed the entrance and continued the dive Pepe turned and motioned back towards them to look at the cavern. The warm water cascaded with the cooler water. A thin veneer had formed around the edge of the cavern. From this angle they could see around to where they had been half an hour ago near the sea fan. It was still swaying in the current capturing little pieces of plankton as they came upon its big hand. Perched on this outcropping they overlooked the whole of the seamount. They could see the western wall drop below them and to their right the jagged blue valley where schools of hammerheads notoriously originated.

Their breaths were calmer during this last part of the dive as they felt a certain amazement overtake and pass through them. The divers swam around the lower ledge of the seamount until they reached the anchor line. Pepe freed the rusted steel wedge and tossed it clear of any other large stones. The divers grouped around the line and proceeded up slowly, sadly. Their bubbles wavered on their lips as time decreed they had to leave the seamount for the surface.

# CHAPTER 33

Gus came sharply to the realization that he was indeed free to do as he pleased, and that was his dilemma. Naturally he believed that there would be "societal penalties" if he did not fulfill certain duties and once again his mind came upon the idea that it was significantly easier to get into something than it was to get out of it.

Experience was his best teacher as he considered how his past actions had led him to his present life. It had been relatively straightforward; he studied, he excelled, and no matter what philosophical view he was now championing, Gus knew by all accounts he was blessed and had lived a charmed life. It was a life where he needed only to develop his innate mental abilities and hone his intellect to what other men couldn't and he was considered successful. This was a clearly defined path. The trail he now approached seemed so liberating, but he knew it was all ideological bullshit until he needed to beg for something.

He wasn't naïve or at least he though he wasn't. It seemed almost counterintuitive to the concept of freedom, but he needed a plan, a plan with some sort of exit criteria that could at least adequately facilitate the dream. Again in his heart he felt the burning desire to leave. It was barely controllable anymore. Gus left the office with a pocket notepad and a pencil.

He walked outside into a blizzard and perambulated along the snow-covered sidewalk to the Park Street T-station. Along its edges an embankment of snow had formed. He opened the door hurriedly and shuffled down the steps. They were dank, cold steps salted to provide traction and steel-plated to provide durability.

Gus boarded the first train that came his way. The redline train destined for Alewife jerked away from the station and skirted along the tracks with the characteristic steel squeal. Gus picked a seat in the front, flipped open his notebook, and started thinking about acceptable exit criteria. He thought about what most people would think about first. He thought whether he had enough money to leave. Again the seamount tugged at his heart and he knew what it was saying.

If he continually debated in his mind how much money he could live on it would always seem like it wasn't enough. That was the law of the rat race; there never was enough money to buy the next big thing. One could work fifty hours only to consume an equal amount, similarly if one worked a hundred hours one consumed just as much in resources. One step predicated another and it became harder and harder to live in a lower caste, to reject the trappings of the material world. Gus pondered the law of the rat race. It seemed inescapable, but was it?

He did a quick summary of his assets and realized he was worth just under $200K liquid. Then he thought about what held him back. Inevitably he thought about debts. And his heart felt heavy and there was no burning in his chest for the seamount agreed. Gus thought about this for a moment. Perhaps only poor health was more restrictive than debt.

He thought about his situation. He owed nearly his liquid worth in debt. His position, education, and lifestyle had come at a price, as they always do. He quickly scratched out a couple figures, made some annotations, and circled the number 16 on the pad. Without too much heartache he could reasonably eliminate the negative debt he accrued and walk away from his current position debt-free in 16 months. His mind leaped back to his original idea of not having enough money to leave.

What if he or Meghan got sick? What if they couldn't find even minimal work in Mexico? There were a lot of "What if?" questions floating around in his mind. And yet, the seamount burned again. What if, it asked him, he never lived his life? What if then? He struggled to put his arms around this. It was hard to believe he wasn't living his life today. What was all of this nonsense he was thinking? Again it burned, but much worse this time for the lie he had told himself was so vile. Gus silently nodded his head in agreement with the seamount. He looked around the train and let the sound of the subway fill his mind. It hummed. He thought and thought some more, then he wrote and time passed.

When he had put the finishing touch on his list of exit criteria it all seemed to focus on one central concept, namely to ditch the Joneses, grab his cash, and head to Mexico. Gus looked up. He had reached the end of the line. He stayed on the same train while it idled at Alewife for new passengers. Slowly the train filled then jerked away back to Park Street.

It seemed to take twice as long to get back to the office now that he had his mind made up. Gus exited the T station and walked back into the vestibule of his firm. The sky was still tossing flakes of snow in the air and comfort of the office beckoned him. He edged past the secretary and almost made it to his office when one of the firm founders spotted him. "Conflict" his mind thought.

"Hey Gus," Herman Myers waved out his hand to Gus while clutching his daily organizer tight by his side. Gus put on that fake smile he had grown so accustomed to wearing lately.

"Hi Herman, what's going on?" Gus asked a question he wanted no answer to.

"Going on, heck what isn't?" Herman put his arm around Gus's shoulder and brought him in closer. He made it a personal point to invade everyone's personal space as often, and intimately, as possible. "Ya know Gus I've got some time off coming up and thought I could get together with you to talk about where you'd recommend going."

Gus had known this type for years; it was what he was so desperately trying to avoid becoming in life. Their lives were generally pleasant, these type of people, except of course that they weren't really alive so to speak. They followed the path of academic excellence, incurred or had their parents incur the debt that requires, and steadily worked their way up. They trudged, fought, trapped, and tricked. Often they succeeded.

They typically vacationed in Hawaii or Disneyland, and had grown mildly independent and somewhat fierce like most everyone else in their generation. Now, they wanted to travel the world. They made it a point to seek the best destinations from the young itinerant travelers who worked for them. But instead of doing the research themselves or learning a culture on their own, these regales sought to pull everything good out of a place from the well-traveled young.

Gus too had followed the ideas of obtaining higher education, but instead of taking the low road he went there and explored, and found in many instances what others would never have found or sought. Obviously the temptation was to spill his guts and start talking with Meyers about all the fabulous places he had been to and the adventures he had experienced and the true friends he'd made by becoming part of a culture. But the burning his heart held him back.

These stories, these adventures, these friendships were only for those who earned them. For those with grit in their teeth and weathered skin. For those people who chose the life of adventure and an empty wallet rather than those who thought they simply could buy the experiences of another with a full wallet.

"Geez Herman, I really don't have too many good recommendations now, given the current travel conditions around the world it's probably pretty dangerous." Gus knew this would work well, simply indicate that things might be dangerous and it usually scared off 90% of the travelers right from the start. It didn't deter Herman though.

"Oh come on now Gus, I've been around you know!" Herman stopped to wink. "Tell me where would you recommend?" His cavalier attitude and enthusiasm almost made Gus talk again, for he sounded like just one of the adventurers, but Gus was rightly cautious again. A regale in sweatpants is still a regale.

"Hmmm…let me think about that Herman." Gus was trying to think of somewhere indiscriminate that would sound snazzy but at the same time not reveal anything at all wondrous. "Well Herman given your resources," and what Gus meant was the virtually limitless flow of cash Meyers had, "why don't you launch a dive expedition in Hawaii on some of the outer islands?"

Meyers' curiosity and eyebrows peaked. He liked the sound of this adventure, and it was clearly well within his capabilities, but yet out on the edge enough to be respected by the Saturday night dinner crowd of his contemporaries. "I like it Gus, I like it!" Herman patted Gus on the shoulder and made his way down the hallway holding his black leather organizer close to his body.

Gus let his eyes follow Herman down the hall. He thought the day organizer glowed red with some unknown agenda. Its leather flushed red like Herman's erratic cheeks, and like a married couple it grew to look like him. Indeed, one could almost correlate the emergence of the day organizer with the fall of the free-spirit.

Here now with the organizer a man's day, month, and perhaps life could be planned, budgeted, and executed. It was filled with numbers that sought to divine the future; phone numbers, financials, and calendar dates. Naturally the thicker the organizer the more important the man; why would an important man have a thin organizer? Herman didn't and it was just as thick as him.

Insidiously the culture and obedient following of the day organizer clan emerged. They traveled much, saw little, and exuded an airy confidence in a product or plan that was surely going to change the world. What a fraud!

Gus thought about what lay ahead for him following in the personal diary of the organizer world. What was the life map ready to fold out for him? Well for one thing he was going to have to take note of his tasks to accomplish to succeed; no one simply succeeded without a plan. The plan was accompanied by action items with little squares next to them indicating completion status. It was like a game really.

The object was to devise the most meaningful sentences with boxes next to them, complete the sentence, and then move on to the next rule set of sentences; a successful day planner was reincarnated with every new rule set to the next level of life, a progressive business reincarnation that presumably lead to corporate Nirvana.

Gus looked across the hall into his office and the day planner waiting for him on his desk. It beckoned him forward. For a task. For an action. For a meeting. For a review. For some piece of his precious time, any piece would due to start. How innocent it looked. Just leather, a zipper, and some paper inside it. Oh, but it was far more than that, and everyone knew it. It was who you were. It was your livelihood! Make a decision without it? Hold a meeting without documenting it here? Complete an action without annotating it here? Preposterous! He pondered the dilemma at length as he stepped into his office; the length of his stride was three feet, so in four steps he had reached and disposed of his problem, at length.

Gus let his heels fall indiscreetly as his door closed behind him. Two worlds tugged at him; one instilled and the other carefully distilled. To be successful in the first he realized the sacrifice society demanded; it demanded his utter and complete dedication to the career. There was no half speed, no "see how it goes," no, it was full throttle or none at all. This game was too dangerous to play at half-speed. The later option required an utter and complete paradigm shift. He would have to turn reality on its heels. In his mind he was already in Mexico and that was the first and primary step; visualization of the transformation. He needed to bend reality to fit his dreams, goals, and life.

He left work that day in a mental quest seeking a balance of independence and dependence. It was not enough to be smart; it was not enough to devote his life to a financial pursuit that would ultimately leave his soul empty. In his mind he grabbed the shining bronze pendulum and swung it back towards society's renaissance. Where were the great adventurers of yesteryear that risked fortunes exploring the world above and beyond what was already known? Who now sought knowledge for its own sake, suffering those trials that inspire humanity? All of that was suspiciously absent in a culture, a society, bent on economic summits whose lofty peaks were mere mounds of paper to be scattered by the wind.

Gus exhaled. He let the breath flow from him and fill the office completely. He was fully exhausted. His willingness to "go there" was intense which made being patient extremely difficult. Cases on his docket seemed to merge. He found himself frequently distracted. More and more his thoughts turned to living in La Paz. He was excited to share his dreams with Meghan, but found only a Dear

Gus letter with a corresponding list and checked box next to it on the fridge when he got home.

# CHAPTER 34

Herman Myer walked past August flush with a fabulous vacation idea, but at the same time held in his mind the reservation that perhaps he could do even better. Of course, naturally he could.

Each step followed the next along the taunt designer carpeting. His step was sure on a padded floor. It cushioned the results of his heavy walk and gave him the protection of a second skin, a second skin that insulated his foot and body from the intense reality that constantly pushed in on him. It was a realty in which he had constructed over his thirty years in law. It wrapped, and turned, and writhed in ways only peers of his latitude could comprehend.

They were the wealthy proletariat content to work for a steady paycheck, medical insurance, and the satisfaction that in the morning their job would most likely be there. They would be there, and there would be there too. Even in the slumps and bumps of economic turmoil that interjected in their daily lives they worked their lingering, jiggling hours. Hours invested not on thought or contemplation but rather lavished on the letter of the law, irreverent for the most part of the spirit of the law, and most assuredly lacking that distinct definition of life, that life was for living and giving.

There was another choice, though, but it was dangerous. Especially dangerous because once one grew in position, and hence salary, "stepping down" in caste was unthinkable! Each house succeeded the other in size, each car more elegant, and each case more prominent.

"Beeeepp!" "Beeeeppp!" A digital alarm clock pulsed in the darkness. The dawn was still an hour away, but Herman woke almost instantly. Was that a nightmare? How would he know? He was one of those people that didn't really enter REM sleep so at the slightest sound of his alarm clock it was simply a matter of opening his eyes from the night interlude. His wife was still sleeping and snorted out incessant snores that always seemed to tunnel into his brain. Herman picked up the bags under his eyes and shuffled into his marble bath (Herman's wife had wanted a house with a his and hers bath so it could hold more of her cosmetics, plus it made it easier for the maid to clean she insisted.)

Herman walked down three flights of stairs in his brownstone until he reached the kitchen. The coffee was ready (he started the pot from the button in the bathroom.) The morning paper was late, so he thumbed through this month's Forbes, absorbed the succinctness of the latest wealth building model, and poured coffee into his Capuchin mug (an antique he acquired in Italy with a bargaining prowess hence unseen.)

Before he took a sip of his second cup of coffee Herman was already in the office. He made it a point of order to be first in the office. He locked the front door behind him and started out ahead of his partners. By the time the secretary arrived to officially open the firm Herman had already put in a solid two hours of briefs, emails, taskers, reminders, re-taskers, and roadmap plans. He was instrumental in getting and keeping the firm's business affairs in order, this he knew.

Herman called it baiting the hooks—he figured by the time the other partners and associates came in the office, not to mention the administrative staff, he had already assigned them their work for the day. At 10 AM he diverted his attention to current event research, the latest law articles, and basically scouring for future business. He intermittently refined taskings send out earlier in the morning. This riding-the-flames-of-hell pace eased into noon. He pulled up on the clutch, eased off the gas, and slid his perpetual motion machine into a double Long Island Iced Tea lunch. It napped his mind but kept his body up. Up for more work in the post-two hour lunch when he started on his third cup of coffee. He prepped the associates on trials, litigated prepared cases, and fought hard into his fourth cup of coffee, just before five. The atmosphere thinned as the afternoon sun fell. The administrative staff finished up their personal business on the internet (of course he got reports monthly on each employee's phone calls and internet activity) and wished him a sarcastic "I got you around my finger" good evening on their way out.

They moved their idleness directly to the local downtown bars where the women sat around in designer clothes purchased on highly inflexible layaway plans riding the top of credit card interest solutions. They were the trend setters who made the scene, worked out in the gyms until their bodies glowed, and went home to continue on their lives. Lives typified by a four-year college education, society-deemed higher IQ, well-read in the book clubs, and well-traveled to Spain or Italy on their biannual trip. The associates arrived later.

They were the larger fish in the sea. Their clothes were a nudge finer, their words louder, and their egos bigger. If the administrators to the regales would stay longer they would eventually see the partners come. The partners made the rounds, shook hands, and feed the egos of their coterie. In five hours they would have to wake up and repeat this cycle again for the 51st week of the year.

# CHAPTER 35

Javier curled the boat's midsection along the current and let it slide into the passing wave. His eyes swept across the expanse of the ocean and fell on the seaweed enveloped rocks they rapidly approached. Javier edged Sea Zephyr over so a pair of women kayaking along the coast wouldn't get caught in the boat's wake. Their backpacks and tents slopped on the bow of their banana yellow sea kayaks.

Pepe disassembled the dive gear and put new tanks on the divers' rigs. They had completed their first dive of the day and now were going to get some rest on the beach. The landscape enthralled the Canadians. It was over a hundred degrees just inland of where they were docking, but on the water it was cooler. Pepe glanced over his back and thumbed Javier to a shaded cavern. The boat's engines cut out and they drifted silently under a ledge that provided relief from the sun. The water was shallow here.

"Ah everyone, I hope the diving was excellent for you. We really had a very special first dive on the seamount." Pepe's eyes were alive with the teeming fish he had seen underwater. He loosened the anchor and let it slop down into the water as his fingers double barreled the rope line.

Pepe lifted his head and smiled at the divers. His small lips naturally averse to pontification said few words. "Yes, yes, so wonderful today. Javier has our lunches. We can just wade over to the beach from here...have a nice little lunch and perhaps a short siesta." Pepe helped the first Canadian into the water and let her slide over the edge and into the waist deep water.

"I'll take the cooler if you'd like," she reached up and motioned Javier for the cooler that had all of their lunches. Javier bent over the boat and steered it into the water. The cooler bobbed along after her.

The divers dipped into the warm sea and made their way towards the beach. Pepe switched out all the yellow aluminum tanks and stripped down to his black swim trunks. The Canadian looked back at Pepe and let her eyes follow the contours of his body as he slipped in the water after her.

Pepe was sturdy in his frame, but lean in difference to the younger Javier's plumpness. He kept so by constant diving and a diet of fresh fruit, fish, and minimal alcohol. He was often quoted a much younger age than he really was. Pepe leapt from the boat and slowly back-peddled his way to the beach. The two gold chains around his neck bounded up and down; the first chain his father had given him when he had completed his primary school and had since been lengthened to account for his growth. The second was from his wife. It bore the signs of never being removed for the once-shinny links had over time eased into a satisfied glaze.

Javier spread a plastic tarp on the sand and anchored it with an assortment of rocks, shells, and stones. He placed the cooler in the center and shimmed open the portable feast. The divers were ravenous as usual and Javier quickly dispensed the food.

They ate heartily then slowed as it became apparent to their bodies that calories were on the way. Javier brought a little pile of food over to Pepe who was under an umbrella propped up in the sand.

"How's it going?" Javier drew up next to Pepe.

"Another wonderful dive on the seamount." Pepe looked across the ocean toward the seamount.

Javier was uncharacteristically quiet for a moment and let the breeze coming from the sea sweep upon him. The sand was moist so it held fast. Waves, little crescent ones, sipped from the shore and trickled back again.

"Pepe, it seems I have some problems with Cervantes again, and this time they originate with my father." Javier came directly to it.

"Well that is no surprise Javier, Cervantes is not fond of the man, although it would be unwise to hold such a grudge," Pepe remarked.

"So you have heard of the tea cup incident?" Javier left his eyes on the ground.

"Indeed. And how long will the old man be against you Javier?" Pepe wondered.

"Indefinitely it seems. I make little strides with Mari but it is useless with that father around."

"It is not you he dislikes Javier...well...I take that back, it may indeed be you he dislikes," Pepe smiled "or it could rather be the mere connection that his daughter has become a woman of age to be on her own. It worries him, and naturally you present an ideal target. What is needed here, I think, is some comparison."

"Comparison? Some challenge where I must prove myself?" His attitude warmed.

"Yes, but rather a man he would accept and then perhaps see all the benefits he offered. You see, to him there is an inbreed loyalty to those of position who live in Mexico."

"Why would I want to find such a competitor?"

"To be the man yourself, of course."

# CHAPTER 36

Gus Merit's hands tapped along the stairwell of his home. He wasn't expecting to have a great escape plan and no one to escape with. He hadn't seen Meghan for over seven months now and only infrequent messages on his answering machine provided some comfort that she was actually still around. He came home now more weary and tired then he had in the past. It was the weariness of a man who had capitulated. Colleagues at work had been sympathetic for the first week and Myers even offered to let Gus have the rest of the week off to get his affairs in order.

Anger had turned to despondency and that actually was slowly dissipating. Somehow he had found comfort in keeping his thoughts together with the idea that his plan, now more than ever, was the right way to go. Rather than being lost he was found and rather then choosing to drown in his sorrow he swam onwards.

Time had taken on a life of its own and seemed particularly content moving at its despairingly slow speed. He worked, he ate, he slept, he worked. He repeated this incessant cycle and gradually time of its own accord changed. A year quickly passed. Gus grew mentally stronger and a touch wiser. His thoughts preceded his words often now and an inner contentment slowly unrolled before him. His mind became sharp and his efforts focused. He deliberately made his thoughts positive, accomplishing ones. Success became a predictive outcome. He was firmly set upon the dream. His only trepidation was the plan. "The plan," it seemed occupied an inordinate amount of time.

Gus mentally debated the merits of his escape plan carefully. He had come to the conclusion that not everything in life quite worked out as planned and to this extent knew that the plan he devised would only hold merit it if was executed; taking the first step was integral. So he took it.

His largest financial holding was his yuppie condo. He had purchased the two bedroom one bath condo in Boston's Back Bay for $320,000 late in 2000, well after the housing boom had crested. Employment was still strong and $100,000 jobs were plentiful. He would be lucky to get the same price in today's market.

Gus put his condo up for sale, furnishings included, at a sub-market price and found it sold within a fortnight. He was able to pull $108,000 in equity from his home, not bad for a fire sale timeline, and pretty much put him at even. Closing would be another month off, but the largest cash item had been secured. Gus made his primary residence the office.

The plan for getting out of work, however, was more difficult. Once again, the time-honored tradition of getting yourself into something you can't get out of was in effect. He had been involved in a sporadic, and apparently ever increasing, amount of litigation on behalf of several clients. The billable hours were soaring but he just couldn't very well give his two weeks' notice, could he?

The solution in this instance, he believed, had to be one of diplomacy. He was a good swimmer, but kept the adage of never burning bridges close to his heart. So with deft insidiousness he slowly transitioned the bulk of his work. It took him the better part of two months to do this, but he didn't leave anyone hanging in the breeze, despite his hair-trigger desire simply to walk out the door.

At the close of eighteen months since developing his plan, Gus gave his two weeks notice. He had been watching the markets for the right time to sell. That time didn't come, so consolidated his finances at a lower price into one basket. His spreadsheet opened on the computer. Gus looked at the balance sheet. He shook his head quietly knowing he had paid almost twice as much for the undergraduate and law school than his current liquid worth indicated. Thirty-two and the majority of his assets were in his head.

Gus traded his car in for a Jeep, packed a single suitcase, and left a letter to Meghan with what he was doing. He enclosed a check for half of his assets, and offered an open-ended invitation. Two weeks later Gus Merit rolled into La Paz, Mexico and started living a new life as a well-heeled bohemian.

# Chapter 37

The sun had crept over the sky by the time the divers had lunched and seistaed. The air had become thick with the afternoon in a groggy slump that stayed with the divers as they packed up their gear and waded now back to the boat. The tide had come in and raised the water to a full standing height. The sea was getting choppy before its time.

"Javier," Pepe scanned the sea "let's go to the sea lion colony for the second dive, the waves are going to make it too rough out to the seamount this afternoon."

An audible sigh characteristic of children wanting to play outside then told to nap was collectively released by the divers hoping to make a second dive at the seamount. Pepe took in the sigh with a smile.

"Well, it's not the end of the world, you know! The sea lions are waiting for us Javier, vamos!" Pepe twirled his right index finger in the sign of a propeller.

They pulled the boat up along the crag. The sea lion colony greeted the divers with barks of welcome that seemed genuinely sincere, save perhaps for the old bull who preferred not to be disturbed and simply barked a warning not to encroach upon his tanning pad.

Lazy in the warmth, the sea lions lay strewn across the hot rocks sunning themselves. Occasionally one slumbered into the water and barked his delight. There were little ones, big ones, and baby pups too. All lounging along a rocky clump a kilometer off the mainland. They were beautiful from afar and rather strong scented from a close.

Even the birds on the island seemed content in their retirement homes. Nests were constructed on ledges offering a panoramic view of the bay below. Only a skilled aviator could successfully build a perch here though, the approach was a notoriously difficult one that had prematurely stripped the feather of many a rookie bird. So it was left to the older birds to mate and raise their last nestlings here.

The nestlings on the sea lion island colony typically stayed longer and grew bigger here as the water was rich with food. The nestlings grew to become great seabirds themselves for in their youth they received twice as much protein as their mainland peers. When they finally did leave the roost they were great big alpha birds. Those that survived the course of natural selection ultimately returned to this palace of nesting in their later years to raise a special batch of eggs themselves. But for now the fledglings simply opened theirs mouths hungrily for the next meal.

Pepe's head scanned the sky and followed a singular bird that circled, circled, then dove. He counted to himself silently. The seconds drew out. Suddenly, a great gush of water overcame the surface as the Kingfisher sprung from the depths with a beautiful silvery prize clenched in her beak.

The rocks themselves seemed alive with this fervor of life. The Canadians were in awe of the beauty, as were Pepe and Javier despite having seen it a thousand times.

The divers geared up in order of their partner entry teams. Pepe was busy getting the group's briefing in as they were pulling on damp wetsuits, the bane of scuba divers worldwide.

Pepe motioned around the colony as he spoke. His words were, as usual, calm and collective despite helping a diver put on a rig, fasten a fin strap, and zip a wetsuit. The common problems that typically aggravated some divemasters were to him trivial formalities that were happily fixed so that everyone could enjoy the dive. It was this same spirit found in the heart of someone doing a job he loved.

"The pups especially enjoy being in the water with humans. You'll soon see who the real master underwater is." Pepe's voice trailed off towards the sea lions lying on the rocks. So fat and so lethargic on land, but a master in the sea he thought. They lived their lives as sea lions do; they played, and they ate fish, and they mated. They fought and, despite Pepe's assurances to the divers, they were eaten by sharks. To humanize their behavior would be false, but then again to sea lionize a human's would be just as false.

One after another the divers flipped off their rock, the boat, and plunged into the sea. They rolled onto an underwater circus filled with the most playful of clowns. The pups circled around the divers. Swimming by them in a flash then suddenly swimming away as if embarrassed by their own boldness. The water here was clear and warm. Pepe took the divers along the island's shoals and through a tunnel that arched above the water.

It rose twenty feet and peaked with sunlight showering the rocky cathedral ceilings. And the walls. The walls were covered with nudibrachs; shell-less snails with freely exposed lungs on the exterior of their body. The blue shawl nudibrach was in some instances as large as a man's hand. They opened their lungs and painted a frieze of all that was beautiful in life. Their lungs radiated orange, yellow, and red polka dots that contrasted sharply with a toned, royal blue body. They were soft to the touch and easily disturbed. It was only by patience and observation that a diver actually could fully enjoy an encounter with this animal, but as with all things both beautiful and useful in life (a rare combination indeed!) it was worth the wait.

The divers completed their circumnavigation of the island and came upon a thin spider crab that was heading for the shelter of an underwater crevice. Its long, skinny legs with oversized knee joints walked funny on the sandy bottom. The spider crab lurched over the rock and was gone, save for two suspicious eyes gazing out from the rock's hole.

Pepe brought the group of divers back up to the surface and Javier wheeled Sea Zephyr around to pick them up. The divers were thrilled and grinning widely the entire ride home, and surprising so was Javier. Pepe didn't say a word but knew already what was to come, it seemed Javier must have made some plan upon their lunchtime discussion after all.

# CHAPTER 38

That night was darker than most. The wind had kicked up something fierce and the entire bay had transformed from placidity to slapping waves. What could be done with the moored boats was done, the others were left to their own device and soon made unhappy trips seaward of their own accord.

Javier was waiting for his father. The diner reservation was for seven o'clock so naturally Javier was there at half past six. He had been summoned in as typical a fashion as always; a courier had left an invitation on his apartment door. Javier wasn't surprised to see it. It had become his time, he reckoned, to meet with his father about "his life." The old man had given Javier time to fetter out the ambitions of his youth and enjoy the pleasantries of a life emancipated by the sea. But now Javier knew his father wanted something more, something that would require the rest of his life pursuing, that style, atmosphere, and culture of living commensurate as a son and future regale.

Javier's day to day living afforded no hint to his privileged class, something his father had purposely tried to accomplish. He wanted the young man to live and grow in the toils of the common man to appreciate what being wealthy, being a regale meant. It meant power and control, and ultimately the money which the respect of millions depended. Rather than send Javier to university in Mexico City or aboard Mr. Vasquez chose to keep him in Baja. Here the boy learned to struggle and sweat.

The value of toil was lost many times on the second or third generation of regales and that was when their status changed. Mr. Vasquez had no intention of that happening. He saw his dynasty growing over years and decades into a future in which a Vasquez would hold the highest political office. He thought long term and executed for those eventualities daily. Now it was time to wean Javier off that life which he now lived and immerse him fully in the roles and responsibilities for which he knew his son was destined.

An imported grandfather clock, dating from the time of Austria's alliance with Mexico, had somehow made its way into Mr. Vasquez's study. It was a lumbering beast with thick hands whose gold tips nearly obscured the numbers to which it pointed. The brass chains fell in neat flows from the clock's crest and piled brazenly on the interior of the glass shell, thrice-replaced.

The clock fit well in the study, a study of European design but executed by Mexican carpenters with native woods. Tough, resilient lumber from the peninsula's interior was carted along unpaved roads, milled, and reformed into a classic study complete with swinging book cases and a matching executive desk that sprawled a third of the twenty foot width of the room.

A humidor kept a box of fine cigars fresh. Javier helped himself. Long, thin strands of smoke rose high into the air and quaffed just above the peaked ceilings. He took long, purposeful breaths and contemplated his situation. He knew he would have to go back into the mainland; that is where they all went eventually for their indoctrination. To Mexico City for several weeks, then on to either New York, Madrid, or Paris for further finishing. He would be gone for two years, minimum. Javier contemplated his fate. He knew what was expected of him and roughly what his father would say. That was certain. He knew what awaited him if he accepted and what awaited him if he refused.

The benefits of accepting were far too generous to refuse; he would be a fool to do so. The terms, of course, are what remained negotiable. He had come to love his current style of living and his father knew it. They talked infrequently as father and sons are prone to do, but talked when the matter of business arose most intensely.

Javier placed the cigar on the ash tray. It puffed red then faded softly into a steady burn. Ashes fell onto the glass until a pinch of them had formed. Javier rolled the cigar in his fingers. He felt his ideas would find a caring ear in his father, if presented correctly. He would give his father the respect he deserved but play his card deliberately and unwaveringlingly; it was all he had to sway the opinion of the older Vasquez. He would agree to all of the his fathers terms on the education in Mexico City and aboard. He would not protest, save to limit the term to two years and the course of study he was to follow would be his alone to choose. The dining bell rang.

Javier snuffed out the cigar and left it in the ash tray. He stood from the fine leather couch and walked across the carpeted wood floor. Javier made his way down the staircase into a fully set dining room complete with half a dozen triple candle holders lit with slender white candles and two bottles of red wine on the table. Mr. Vasquez, senior, opened the adjoining door with a broad smile to see his son suited so tastefully and struck upon him at once in conversation.

# CHAPTER 39

Mr. Vasquez retained a unique interest in science from his university days. Always enamored with the idea of eternal youth, he had in fact devoted much of his spare time focused on that pursuit. For a man so typified by his position in life, that of the PEMEX chief in Baja, he was particularly astute in the field of genetics and had for some time made an undisclosed effort to copyright his DNA. He thought it was a particularly clever thing to do.

He imagined what it would be like to live forever. Indeed, this was a common theme among the regales, to live forever, or at any rate extend their lives to the last possible moment in the absence of an eternal life. Some put their faith in technology, like Mr. Vasquez, for they had long ago renounced religion. Others sought companionship in the company of God. They felt their lives could be graced even further in the vaulted ceilings of heaven.

Mr. Vasquez had personally appeared in church rarely save for the infrequent times it was necessary on state business to keep such an appointment. He had realized that his time on earth was limited and he sought to maximize the power of his earthly influence. All of this spiritual stuff seemed somewhat irreverent. He measured his success on the fruit of his labor. It was this way with the majority of regales.

They hungered for control and power, cannibalizing smaller players to bring themselves added control and power. Eventually though, the apex of the food chain became a tight squeeze and fratricide was a common occurrence. It was a sobering thought. Mr. Vasquez, as the other regales, took every opportunity to dig himself in his niche and remain secure; a sense of security built on the sweating brow of his corporation.

# CHAPTER 40

Seasons and hearts often change together, and with each passing breath August Merit inhaled more life. It gave him strength and vigor he had never known. He lived now on a stretch of land above the main highway in La Paz. It was vacant save for a decaying construction attempt abandoned many years ago, perhaps left by a man like himself who had noticed the natural beauty of this land and had grown to love it in his dreams.

Gus began where the previous owner left off. He furnished the new place with an odd assortment of pieces discovered in the city. Gus arranged a perfectly reasonable living area within days of his arrival. He fancied that all good things in life were free and that it was no leap to champion the life of a noble bohemian as the pinnacle of existence.

It was in his happiness that Gus noticed later that he wasn't thinking about being happy. He simply lived his life and occupied his time accomplishing his goal. He had succeeded in exiting his previous situation by sticking to his goal and eliminating distractions that came along. He reflected for a moment on his goal, of he and Meghan living together here on the Baja peninsula and being what he loved.

It was after his initial acclimatization, which was followed by the brainstorming period, that followed his wife's return. Meghan had passed the months of their separation with initial satisfaction in knowing the freedom she now had but barring the occasional interlude of a man she had come to find what she was missing was what she had had. She had an epiphany of her own, one that required introspection, courage, and ultimately decision. What would he say she wondered? What would his reaction be?

She had received his note on her lunch break two months ago and further word arrived that he had refurbished an abandoned stucco house overlooking the old highway. He relayed his experiences, in particular the trouble he had in learning the language and the interesting customs he was continually being exposed to. How, she wondered, could he have such presence of mind and clear intentions to still contact her?

But even this was part of his plan, in a reflectionary way. His trials now were ones of spirit rather than financial, it was a truer calling he now found himself pursing. Not the impetus to follow the rest of the herd prodded by the regales but to break the collective consciousness and step aside and decide for himself what path he would choose. He chose his strategy and executed. While not necessarily the perfect plan, he was aware, that the luxury of time did not always correlate with perfect results. So he placed his bet with the Mexico plan and found his home welcoming him more every day.

In his conversation, in his mannerisms, and the intonation of his letters Meghan could feel he had become one of the few people in this world that follow their dreams and actually accomplish them. And it attracted her far more than she could have anticipated.

Her situation was fundamentally the same as his; barring the fact that she didn't have the high income level he did to affect the exit strategy. Rather, she was burdened with both school and some personal debts that necessitated her stay. Or did it? She thought about her options and wondered how long she would indeed follow this path.

It was an easy excuse, she thought, to rationalize staying in Boston. But then she came upon the realization that this could be the same position she'd be in another one, five, or ten years. Gus recommended she pack only the necessities in an overnight bag, pay all the debts she could with the check he had left her, and leave. But could she actually just walk out? What was the societal implication if she abandoned the established work ethic and in essence defected? Was she somehow entitled to live the life she wanted? Was there some sovereign right allowing one to live life to its fullest?

Meghan smiled to herself and packed her things the next morning. She withdrew the cash she had on hand and purchased a one-way ticket to La Paz, leaving the majority of her clothes, furniture, and things in place. A simple "thank you" note was left on the counter along with her keys for the landlord. Meghan left the city with her most important asset, her freedom.

A plume of acidic black smoke rose as the tires screeched to a halt in La Paz. Gus was waiting in the terminal. He gave her a hug, picked up her two bags (one of which was entirely filled with summer shoes) and for a very long time they just smiled at each other as they walked home.

# Chapter 41

Cervantes had grown wise to Javier's advances and made it a point of honor in staving off these ingenious, rarely successful, maneuvers at his daughter. In time these faded as Javier left La Paz on some crazy mission. People said he had an awakening; Cervantes knew he had finally just gone crazy and was glad to be rid of the pesky nuisance. The reality was neither of course.

The mosquito had been gone for over two years and Cervantes' vigilance ceded ever so slightly. It was his fortune, however, to be introduced as of late to a gentleman caller who was from the mainland of Mexico.

He was a gentleman for several reasons, principal amongst these being that he followed Cervantes view of the world in terms of tradition. He was to all accounts of noble birth and had acquired his fortune as of late from a textile operation that farmed a new sort of particularly drought resistant cotton. Or was it heat resistant? Cervantes forgot the details, but knew the specifics. The image of this man projected itself in Cervantes' mind until it became as common as the thought of crafting clay in his hands.

Luis d'Orro came upon La Paz as his supposed fields of cotton grew upon the land, he seeded himself first in the minds of the people and then bloomed in their hearts. In a torrid of words, his reputation seemed to precede his every move. He wore the most fashionable clothes and spoke with the etiquette of a Spanish gentleman. His mannerisms were always tactful and his imminent rise in station was largely due to sustained rumor. It was only a matter of time before whispers of Luis d'Orro reached Mari's delicate ears. His name and his story were fragrant scents that intoxicated her dreams, and those of most every woman in La Paz.

Due to his large tracks of land and the larger responsibilities still of his position, Luis d'Orro didn't always have time to return to La Paz. His comings and goings were a mystery and only added to his appeal. He came and went at will with hardly a mention of his coming or a hint of his departure.

Of its own accord, or perhaps it was started by someone, it came to be known that Luis d'Orro had walked by Fresh Fruit Ice Cream and had gazed upon the most perfect creature. There was much ado in the same town as friends, and those who claimed they were friends, sought Cervantes' reaction to this.

Rather than being shocked, Cervantes was surprisingly flush with excitement. His luck and reputation had significantly improved since the teacup incident and the departure of Javier; he was eager to shore up more respect from his card playing amigos. He enjoyed the rumors that reached his ears and especially enjoyed becoming a de facto celebrity. In short order, with the buzz coming before the bee, Cervantes received a dinner invitation.

It was constructed of fine paper stock embossed in a sweeping calligraphic font; there was even a short menu with the enclosed response letter! Cervantes peered close to the letters, as his vision dimmed by the day. Long days at the PEMEX plant had clouded his eyes with the blur of repetition at close distances. He relied now more and more on his sense of touch. And while he suffered a blow to his pride regarding the teacup incident his creations were becoming legendary.

Their elaborate designs were executed flawlessly. His vigor awoke in the morning like a small volcano and crested just after noon. It was during these four to six hours that some of Mexico's finest ceramics were being crafted. Slowly the pieces started to disappear off his shelves. The tourists, both Mexican and Americans, no longer were pensive about their purchases; they bought and bought. On all fronts Cervantes had finally reached a period of contentment unbeknownst to him and with the arrival of Luis d'Orro he felt confident his daughter's security would be guaranteed.

# CHAPTER 42

Security versus passion, a decision that more often than not determines a man's health and happiness in life. More and more Gus was beginning to understand the implications of giving up his world of security in which he had obtained a position in the upper echelon. Getting to that level had taken years because it took years to acquire that specific special knowledge. Society, in general of all societies, rewarded higher education (specifically specialized education) with higher salary and greater esteem. But this higher knowledge was tricky, for not every splintered knowledgebase was rewarded equally.

It came to be via economic evolution that the highest paid members of society were the ones that helped make money for other people. It was the preeminent rise in the merchant class that led to the concurrent establishment of nation-states to protect, foster, and grow these businesses. Society placed considerable value on these businesses.

This concept of value was particularly troubling to Gus who had after a time adopted a different philosophy. It was his belief that the secondary and ternary markets were indeed, of their own merit, the driving force behind man. It was the arts, music, and the very classics which served to strengthen and nurture a culture. This presumption further defined his belief in the theory that ultimately it was the ternary market, the impetus to create, that everything else revolved around.

These dreams came to him at auspicious times, such as when the fire on the beach was dying and only embers glowed. That was when he thought best. It was then he compared the different life goals, and in particular the security versus passion belief. He felt particularly enlightened since the awakening he had experienced on the seamount. It was a force that had gripped his entire body and shook his collective consciousness awake.

He marveled at the strength and depth the seamount had had on him. He had given up his career and fundamentally changed his life. He realigned what was important. Meghan too had changed since she came down to Mexico. The anxiety of the daily grind was replaced with a pleasant yearning to live, and increasingly to give. The peaceful climate and hospitable culture happily chipped away at years of societal establishment cemented on her psyche.

Gus learned to embrace the belief of all things in moderation, and he moderated his freedom so it too did not become distasteful. When he wasn't helping Pepe on the dive boat, since Javier had become Luis d'Orro and Luis d'Orro married Mari and moved to the mainland, Gus made himself work long hours in harsh conditions. In two short years he had developed a particular pride in doing the most menial tasks.

Nothing was below him. He became a hired hand of sorts with the local farmers and fisherman. The longer he lived in La Paz the greater his reputation was amongst the populace. He gave freely of his time and talents. They accepted him as their native son and even helped derail a measure that would have had him pay back property taxes on his land. It was established that the renovations he had performed and the consequent labor in the city paid for any back taxes.

Gus's hair had grown long and wavy like the sea, he bent it back into a little pony tail. The tips blonded in the sun and when he let his hair loose he resembled a lion. Besides his hair, the most obvious difference was in his physique. Days spent scuba diving and working on the water had hardened him. He was toned and healthily tanned. His step had changed too.

It was no longer the step of a man who was making haste in every direction. It was the motion of a man content to live his life as he saw fit. The whole premise of wasting time had become incomprehensible; moments were simply enjoyed like ripe fruit. And as they say people who age together start to look like each other so too was the case with Meghan and Gus.

Meghan's hair grew longer too and her fair complexion was bronzed. She carried a wicker basket to the morning market and chatted with the shoppers about their children's English lessons. She worked two shifts a day three days a week and spent the remainder of her time enjoying the garden atop their hilltop home. Many days she drove around the countryside in a dune Buggy discovering worthwhile beach picnic spots. Meghan too had become a firm believer in the powers of the seamount and returned there often. She said it reinvigorated her soul and made it a point to recommended it to any divers she met.

The seamount had the distinct ability to simultaneously calm and infuse passion. Pepe said that was what happened when lava shot up from the center of the earth and vented into the cool ocean; the water molded pure passion into an undersea sanctuary whose creative enery was so strong it changed lives.

# CHAPTER 43

For a long time the photographer had enjoyed his solace and took pleasure in publishing his pictures. His photographic career had experienced a mercuric rise and it all seemed linked to the pictures he published those years ago about Baja.

The photographer had taken several rolls of film that captured the essence of pristine adventure that so many people sought in life. The shots were remarkable. They conveyed the visual beauty of the land and also had the presence of mind to illustrate in the mind's eye a dream. And that was what the people loved. Months after he returned from diving the seamount, the photographer found a dive journal interested in his photography.

The photographer submitted his spread on Baja after several tantalizing pictures of the area were positively reviewed by the photographic editor. The editor bought the entire spread and promised commissions on all shots distributed. It wasn't long before the photographer realized just how good his pictures were. The financial faucet opened and a steady stream of cash made its way to the photographer's hands. He decided to put more effort into his passion and took classes at the University of New Mexico. They proved to be educational, but yet they were above water. So like any great athlete, he sought his playing field elsewhere.

The photographer used his talents part-time to spring together enough cash to make his way to Monterey, CA. The home of Steinbeck's heroes was a fertile ground for this budding photographer. The photographer was at once diving off the coast and photographing the panoply of anemones, sea stars, and pelagics that made these cool waters their home. He dove daily and made his residence with two other students, one of business and the other of pleasure, in a rented clapboard house three blocks removed from the ocean.

It wasn't long before the photographer had studied enough, and flooded three cameras in the process, that he had assembled a visually compelling collection. The photographer was able to open a small show simply on the merits of this initial portfolio. The show opened to rave reviews and lasted the entire summer. Print sales and licensing rights crested. The photographer had reached that point of being a local celebrity where one could embrace the status and subsequently follow a slow artistic descent into oblivion or reject the coming stardom, leave the area, and reinvent himself as an even a greater success. Naturally, the photographer chose the latter path.

He packed his cameras, left an extra month's rent, and departed Monterey with no forwarding address save "return all mail" written by hand and taped to his post box. The photographer boarded a plane to Southeast Asia where he heard there was a rich underwater land ready to be photographed.

And through this all he fondly thought back on his first meaningful photographs. He often wondered just what it was about the seamount that sparked such a fire in him and his work. Whatever it was, he knew, was inspiring.

The people that had seen his pictures in Monterey knew it too and wanted to get close enough to him to absorb more of this energy. But it was not something to be taken, rather it was something to be blown in the wind like a dandelion. So he blew the magic in the air and brought the beauty of the sea to the lives of so many more people.

# CHAPTER 44

American Airlines flight 27 from Los Angeles to Honolulu landed softly as a 747 can. The plane taxied along the runway for several minutes until it got to its gate. Freddy looked at the control panel as the passengers deplaned. A lonely can of Coke rolled across the aisle as the last passenger left. Jack smiled over and gave Freddy a high five.

They finished the last flight of their careers together and now were going to celebrate. The "dynamic duo" of the trans-Pacific 747 flight had been flying now for over twenty years and scheduled this flight as their last. With retirements secure they felt the world was no longer on their shoulders. The pressure seemed to relax as the throttle fell back and all the lights dimmed.

Leis fell on their shoulders as they left the cockpit and were escorted down the flight line to the terminal. An interesting question was now upon them. They were of the typical retirement age and each had saved a nest egg. The plan seemed simple, as any good plan will, they would live off their guaranteed airline retirement plan and the nest egg.

Time had been kind to the pilots and they were still fully in control of most of their capabilities, dulled, but still fundamentally in control. Bad knees, backs, and eyes aside they remained of sound positive attitude which made all the difference. Freddy had been married, on and off, now for over twenty years to three women. He decided at this point his safest move was to live and enjoy life with his present wife. His advantage, and Jack's too, was that they could travel for free on most flights around the world. This was a tremendous asset which gave them liberty to see and experience a host of things many people never would.

Jack, in comparison to Freddy, had been married to the same women now for twenty-seven years. His plan was similar to Freddy's in that he wanted to take things a lot slower; as it was they worked half a month. His idea of the good life was to hunker down somewhere warm, sleep the mornings away, and fish from noon to dusk. He was also planning to do some light flying to legitimize his lifestyle.

The two longtime flyers meet up that night at Duke's to share a Mai Tai. The sunset was long and drawn out. It covered Waikiki's vast expanse of sand, shore, and ABC stores. Talk fell on retirement as it always does when the sun is falling into night.

"Twenty years in an eye blink, huh Jack?" Freddy stirred his drink to the ukuleles and heard the ice tumble into the glass.

"It's funny, when we were young we really just wanted to fly all the time. Now it seems like all anyone is concerned about is when they're going to retire."

"Yep, it's a retirement culture rather than a work for life culture." Freddy motioned over to the waitress he needed a refill for himself and Jack. Jack shifted his weight in his chair.

"You don't see the 'proud to be at work attitude,' more of a 'glad to get out of here' mood." Jack slowly shook his head.

"Jack, the problem is that folks don't enjoy what they're doing. Some of that is from their own attitude, but a lot of it comes from the fact that there are just so many mind numbing jobs out there. We're the lucky ones mate." Freddy let his gaze follow the hostess.

"Yep, can't agree more with you." Jack sipped, rather than drank, his drink.

The two buddies looked up at the TV screen in the bar. Their eyes both focused on the CNN screen's ticker "AMR, Parent Corporation of American Airlines, cuts all Pilot Retirement plans in effort to keep company out of bankruptcy." The two pilots looked at each other, picked up their Mai Tai glasses almost in sync, and toasted each other.

If there were two things they lived by it was checklists and chance. The lose of their retirements was an example of chance gone wrong. Their profession was notoriously detailed in what to do, but it was the development of the instinct of what to do when things weren't written that separated the average flier from the skilled aviator. And Freddy and Jack were skilled aviators.

It had taken years of precision training and odd luck to hone their mental ability. Some claimed this presence of mind was innate, the very cocky of course, while other said it was something learned over time, the very timid. It was, in fact, a fusion of the two that people either chose to activate and learn from in their lives or not. On a similar note, and one played surprisingly little, is the allegory to immigrants. Millions of immigrants did it, accepting defeat each and every day.

They came to this country willing to pay any price to survive. They often succeeded in both, but over time the raw urge and power of the immigrant was chiseled away by the comforts of a society bent on making everyone a whole of the system. The immigrants motto was survival which ultimately followed Maslow's hierarchy of needs, and once accomplished reverted to living in contentment rather than pursuing dreams; that life was meant for the living became a side note.

Pilots and immigrants for some reason were two groups, and perhaps the best would be an immigrant pilot, who innately knew a person's knowledge base and skill set furthered their lives, but most important survivability trait, the ability to adapt, that either saved someone or left him in ruin.

So the pilot's celebrated their twenty-year retirement that wasn't a retirement by any means. They drank the night away and woke in varying stages of consciousness the next morning. Whether Jack or Freddy knew it by name or simply just used this skill they developed, it served them well. At breakfast the next morning their spirits were surprisingly upbeat.

"Alright, so that's a huge hit to the retirement plan!" Freddy was having a particularly strong mimosa to kill the hangover.

"Yep, kinda hard to recover from a hit like this. The wife is definitely not going to like it. Looks like a heck of an opportunity to start up that small flying service I was interested in doing."

"Yeah mate," Freddy was grinning cheek to cheek now, "you'll be alone doing it too. No way she's going to go along with that scheme of yours!"

"You'd be surpised I think. Pretty good team ya know, she's almost done with the nursing program. Don't think I'll get too much resistance going for it." Jack finished up his coffee and looked around the dining room.

Maybe he was still drunk and somewhat extremely alert now, but it seemed like every couple in the buffet fell into two categories; ones on their honeymoons or those about to see their last moon. And this seemed strangely similar to life; that its enjoyment fell into two categories. The first being the early energy-filled years and the second being the glowing embers of what was. And "what was" was the years upon years spent freely giving life to the regales. Freely giving the regales life, it was a sobering thought that narrowed the focus of Jack's mind.

"So what are you going to do about this setback of ours Freddy?" Jack pushed over the basket of table bread to Freddy.

"Don't really know. Thing is flying is great, I mean I wouldn't have done it for so long if I didn't think so but I'm ready you know?"

"So what you're thinking?" Jack wasn't expecting Freddy to straighten up so quickly.

"I'm thinking maybe I go to medical school." Freddy threw the comment out like a dart.

Jack raised a single eyebrow. "Medical school?"

"Yep, something I always wanted to do. I've got an ample share of cash stored up and figure I can finance a fair share as well. Not really interested in flying around all over. At least not for a while."

Jack tapped his index finger on his temper and asked Freddy in a face all too serious "Do you have the intelligence to get in?"

Freddy smirked and buttered his roll. "I've got plenty of field experience with the human body, mind you not always spreading a cure."

Jack chuckled and they left the table with a nice tip for the hostess who only bothered to fill their coffee cups once.

# CHAPTER 45

Lisa's scar didn't fade with age. It was still as sharp, jagged, and red as the day the whale brought her below the surface of the ocean. She ran her hand along the length of it. Simply feeling it brought back the memory of getting it. She wore her shorts shorter now and cared little of the implied stigma of the scar. Lisa went from job to job for her landscaping business in her Jeep Cherokee with forest green "Loreto Landscaping" advertised on the doors.

She had become particularly adept at her work, the kind of skill realized by those who truly love what they do. Lisa could cultivate the natural xenosphere into something more than it was. Her skill in the use of a shovel, manure, and local faunas routinely transformed piles of dirt and weeds into little Edens.

For several weeks now Lisa had been working on a protected garden overlooking the sea. The property had a sweeping feature about it that dangled some land over a cliff like a breaking wave. Lisa structured the garden to fade into the view of the ocean; thick, rich cacti moved away from the main property and dwindled to patches of wild flowers. Butterflies often rose from the sea mist and decorated the flower patches with their shimmering wings.

The padrone of the property was a Mexican rancher who was particularly fond of useful beauty, such as landscaping, and in particular Lisa. She found herself often under his watchful eye as he hoofed it about the property on his painted horse.

Giamo Torez was one of a rising generation of Mexican farmers and ranchers on the peninsula who had embraced Americanized techniques for agriculture and nodded in quiet agreement to husbandry practices already known for years.

Giamo was the only son of a large family that had staked their claim in Baja at the turn of the century. His father's father was a stout man who had survived the rigors of life and died proud, old, and happy on his property. He was fortunate enough to have seven sons, but it was Giamo's father who had inherited the ranch.

The turn of events had been strange and tumultuous. The two oldest brothers had fought their way into American citizenship only to die in WWII. Giamo's father was the third son and outlived the rest of his brothers. He had a knack for almost anything he did in life and the size and renown of the ranch was due in large part to his luck and labor. He was keen to acquire land in the years of drought and sold parcels in the booms. In this fashion he had stockpiled considerable resources and was careful to hold his currency hard.

Giamo's father had been particularly suspect of paper money because everything of value he knew was heavy and vast. So he kept his growing wealth in gold or silver and as he grew older and the metals tarnished he began to purchase more and more land closer to the ocean. Ultimately he bought right up to the present surf where Giamo was conceived.

Born into the 1960s by a mother who raised her son proudly in the rich traditions of his country, Giamo exemplified the lifestyle of a Mexican ranchero. Giamo had two sisters, both of whom married young and had started strong families of their own in Baja. Giamo, however, had stayed single. It was a peculiar choice for a man that could and did have his choice amongst the women of the area.

His reputation and influence was strong enough to attract the daughters of the mainland, yet he remained uninterested until he was thirty, and only mildly interested past that age. He was never taken by that certain lust that snares men, Giamo was nimble with his feet and walked cautiously. His chosen life was one of acceptance and reflectance. It became apparent though, that recently Giamo had indeed tip-toed next to the snare and in fact admired it greatly. It interested him and teased his mind. It was a sticky and sweet trap that beckoned him to step further. And so he did.

Giamo began to take a personal interest in the ever-expanding services he requested of Loreto Landscaping. It was no longer enough just to watch from his mount on the steed, but rather he immersed himself personally in the labor. And so this quintessential bachelor walked freely into what he had always thought suspect and proudly emerged a married padrone rich in prosperity on all fronts. There was even a whisper of growing grapes for wine in the rancher's ear.

# CHAPTER 46

Meghan wiped the grime off of her face and realized once again they didn't have enough money for the grocery bill. She put Billy on the counter in his soiled diaper and proceeded to put back the least essential items until the she was left with milk, bread, and eggs. The departure south wasn't without its difficulties she had begun to realize. The standard of living she enjoyed in Boston had dropped precipitously and she often wondered how they endured in La Paz with so little income, and now she endured the perfect world for what was beginning to take shape, with her manic husband and her colic son.

Meghan snapped her eyes open. She took a double take of the house. Yes, everything was all right. Billy was sleeping in her arms and she knew Gus was diving today. Poverty. Occasionally she let this thought creep into her mind.

She knew they were financially stable, but it was hard to tell people who wouldn't listen just how possible it was to live life on simpler means. The family ate healthy meals daily. They were prepared at home with love, and increasingly some direction. Esperenza had taken Meghan under her wing and passed many of her mother's secret recipes to Meghan with a wink.

Billy dressed in clean clothes devoid of any overt advertising and further snubbed those articles manufactured by children just years older than himself. Make no doubt, she knew, this was not a lifestyle change for the faint of heart, or the faint for that matter. The living was not easy in the sense that everything was provided, or could be readily obtained whenever, wherever. Necessity indeed proved to be the mother of innovation. It was a Mexican trait, a matter of national pride, to fix the unfixable and improve the unimprovable.

Life moved at a natural pace, a pace congruent with natural laws. The very aspects of humanity purported to be so prized and privileged; the afternoon siesta, the laughter of a family, the freedom of crowds on a beach all came naturally here and free. Free from scorn, envy, or jealously.

Make no doubts though, there was work to be done, laborious sliver-in-the-hands work. Work that dripped blood and tears, but it was the manual labor accustomed to man. He relished it. Working with his hands, working outdoors, and working in the sprit of a team. The richness of family united them all though, for a man working here had a family and so did his boss and so did his. The hierarchy remained, and was evident in daily activities, but it was a mild hierarchy that often took the form of a loose democracy.

The seascape panned open as the sun rose from the sky. Gus was packing the gear for the day. The bulk of yesterday's work was complete. He erected a small beam church in La Paz that had previously succumbed to a combination of poor structural design and time. The foundation had eased into the earth below it and the wooden body had sagged into a burdensome heap.

Esteem had grown wildly in Gus's heart and his labor was the proof of this acceptance. Reluctance in accepting him to the inner circle of La Paz was replaced with a warm fondness for the gringo. His jokes seemed funnier and his work respected. Gus felt the difference in their mannerism toward him. It had taken six years of living in the city, but perhaps the greatest acceptance of him came from the birth of his son. There is something to say of changing lanes in life and settling somewhere new, and it is another to decide that a place is fit for a family.

Meghan had stayed with her teaching. A young woman with a baby that chose to bring the child to class, especially one as sleepy as Billy, was not frowned upon in La Paz. Indeed, despite the mainland's conservative tilt and La Paz's reflection of it many things in Baja were altogether different. Perhaps it was the Mediterranean climate that eased the attitudes and softened the political conscience.

Today, though, Gus was diving. He had assumed more and more responsibility in the diving business. Pepe dove less frequently and made more trips over the countryside talking with people. He would drive the old F150 Javier left him to the ranches and sit to talk with the ranchers. He talked about the Mexico of their heritage and told them stories of the peninsula they had never heard. He relished in their surprise. He spoke candidly about the future and the need to adapt to a world bent on growth that often grew in the wrong direction.

Pepe's name preceded him as he rambled about the countryside bringing families together and talking with them. With age, his laughter and joy in life overflowed. He realized what he had become and shared generously of his life with who he could. When he dove he spoke with the divers, who to a large extend came from afar to dive in his land. But rarely did the farmers or ranchers come to La Paz to dive the seamount. And as is often the case when something great is close to you it is not accepted for how truly great it is. So he sought the Mexicans with whom he lived and they shared their life on the land with him.

The farmers and ranchers naturally were different, they knew about animals, soil and the earth. For many of them the sea was simply a transit lane. In their blood was the earth, the very earth the seamount had long ago deposited on the peninsula. Dark, volcanic earth that retained its constitution even with the drying wind that swept across the peninsula in the summer. The land was rich beyond their dreams and the farmers took a liking to Pepe's exploits and his stories.

They were true Mexican tales that they could only remember faint words of their parents telling them when they were children, but this man knew them all. Word for word, Pepe would look into someone's eyes and start reciting a story he had long since forgotten in the very sands he grew, lived, and would die.

# CHAPTER 47

Three lazy years passed and of its own desire, as things often do, a consortium of the Mexicans decided it was high time to pool their collective knowledge into a museum of sorts.

Fanfare of the situation grew to the point where naturally Cervantes took it upon himself to bring the project to the city. His leadership, eminently lacking in officiality, was immediately accepted on behalf of a loose circle of farmers, ranchers, and reputable card players. Cervantes began at once in gathering signatures, for what purpose he wasn't quite sure, but for some reason signatures always seemed to be needed.

In short order 25,000 signatures were raised from La Paz's 20,000 adults. It was unanimously decided that a heritage site of grand proportions was to be established. A humbled but equally grand site was decided upon when the government application for funding returned to Cervantes without a single peso.

The consortium agreed that the best course of action was to remodel an existing structure. Several ideas were put forth including using the recently raised Church, but that was vetoed by the vast majority of the consortium, including the member who brought it up, on the grounds of immorality; immorality of what the heritage site would include vice actually using the church building to house it. Cervantes paced late into the night on the floor of his pottery barn searching for an answer to this dilemma.

The pressure of concentration only served to heighten his level of stress, in fact Cervantes' funeral was held in the recently raised church a week later with great sorrow by the residents of La Paz. His health had neither been fading nor was he suspect of any particular disease so naturally the blame fell on the government for their refusal to fund the heritage site.

It was only a fitting tribute to Cervantes that it was universally agreed that his pottery shop would indeed become the sight of the heritage center.

Mariposa fluttered in from the mainland upon hearing the news of her father's death. In her arms she cradled a little girl that surpassed even her beauty, and walking in step with her was Luis d'Orro who had come into his own. The family was finely dressed and the procession of flowers was not soon forgotten.

# Chapter 48

For many years now it has been an oral tradition of the man who was two men. His name as the rough and ready youth who dove at the seamount was Javier. He lived with this name by day for many years, but strode down another path when he returned to La Paz one evening. It seemed like only Cervantes had never known this communal secret.

Mari's will dictated that the little pottery shop, which had so much history in just its timbers, would serve as the city's renowned heritage site. Many of Cervantes things were kept in place as they were and added a rustic charm to the newly minted heritage site. Pepe and Esperenza took it upon themselves to model the new Hacienda Cervantes. It didn't take long for them to transform the once quiet pottery shop into a bustling heritage site that the citizens of La Paz short-while decided needed a christening.

It was an ordeal that generated much fanfare. The street signs, whose very nature was questionable in La Paz, became fully functional poster boards for the launch of the heritage site. Gus and Meghan were assigned the job of decorations. They made arrangements with the local paper mill to keep the pulp shavings which were turned into confetti by the hundred pound. Gus contacted several of his acquaintances in the Mexican military who ran second jobs as firework specialists to perform a firework show the evening of the opening. Theirs was sometimes a dangerous job as the fireworks were derived of expired military artillery, distilled to seemingly safe levels, and repackaged as fireworks.

Esperenza gathered the ladies of La Paz together in what became the largest food fiesta the town had ever known. A full week before the christening both sides of the main boulevard were filled with wood of merchant stands. Preparations came to a head and were almost singularly destroyed, however, when the federal government received word of the fiesta.

A bout of legal wrangling ensued. At points the federal government was threatening martial law, but Pepe came to the rescue and called upon his numerous contacts in the federal government, including Mr. Vasquez, to quell the situation by letting the Federal Government officiate the opening and dedicate Hacienda Cervantes. In addition, Pepe was able to work a grant of ten thousand pesos and ratification of the city's government dedicating the new building as Hacienda Cervantes.

The night of the fiesta was especially clear. The pink heavens themselves wanted a window into the party. Hundreds of people filled the streets clothed in bright colors and full smiles. Children ran around the merchants and some played on the beach with sparklers. Roasting chili, chicken, and corn waffled in the air just before the smell of cooking beans overtook the nostrils.

It was between the first and third bottle of tequila that the fireworks display lit the night sky. Chinese inspired and Mexican manufactured rockets flew well beyond conventional firework ranges and exploded high in the sky with resounding "booms!" There were occasional duds, which lifted off the barge, teetered, and fell into the ocean. Many of these subsequently exploded underwater and large burps of seawater intermingled with the explosions in the sky.

The crowd had swelled over the course of the night and neighboring cities had emptied their houses in anticipation of the fiesta. With each passing minute the fiesta's reputation grew in intensity. It wasn't until the sun began its arduous task of climbing over the sea that the fiesta cooled. Many people laid on the beach sleeping in blankets, many more slept on the dock in various states of dress.

Although the Mexican Federal Police attended in large numbers, their presence was principally one of appearance. It was always the government's contention that public gatherings and alcohol created the impetus for revolution. No large fights broke out, the belligerent drunks were rounded up and thrown together in jail, and the thefts that occurred were of such a petty nature that the entire town came to the realization of just how good citizens they were. This only added to further celebration for Hacienda Cervantes, a celebration he watched fondly from above.

# CHAPTER 49

In no uncertain terms the christening of Hacienda Cervantes was a tremendous success. When the sobriety of life fell again upon La Paz peoples' minds reminisced about the christening in terms of organization, execution, and principally enthusiasm. All minds thought of Pepe. His impetus in bringing the community together occurred first on an individual nature then all at once on a larger level.

With the passage of days, it came to be that these individuals shared amongst themselves the thoughts and spirits of their ancestry. The unfettered Mexicana of their birth resounded in their hearts as a sense of pride that was far more valuable than what was being exported incrementally to the United States as cheap labor. Conversation thick with their creative labor infused the richness of their lives, children, and the very way they lived. The significance of Pepe's wisdom was not lost on the collective conscience of La Paz. Steadily throughout the southern state, especially in the remote communities, Pepe's sowed seeds grew. And still he dove.

Pepe dove when the sea was rough and dove when it was so flat the water reflected the sun's rays perfectly back to it. Gus had transitioned from his previous activities and now worked exclusively on Sea Zephyr Too guiding a widening pool of divers to the seamount with Pepe.

Pepe let Gus drive the boat now. He explained to Gus the correct way a divemaster needed to show the seamount. For Pepe being a divemaster was the pinnacle of scuba diving; even more important than being an instructor. Pepe felt that the divemaster was the one who taught the divers what the sea, atmosphere, and soul were all about. An instructor taught the students the accepted practices and rote techniques that formed the basis of their education, no doubt an invaluable service, but being a divemaster was all about finishing. And in finishing the final product Pepe liked to quote his friend Cervantes "sculpt with care and most importantly deliver carefully" what the seamount was and how to channel that energy into positive action.

It was no easy task to assimilate; indeed it had taken Pepe decades just to reach that inner calm he felt and learn how to transfer the seamount's creative energy to others. Gus had the right clay to mold though, and Pepe knew it from the beginning. In the span of seven years Gus had internalized the significance of Pepe's words and actions. His trust extended further than safeguarding just the divers, Gus realized the responsibility he was inheriting and accepted what he had become; the chosen one to succeed Pepe.

The responsibility freed him. His life now focused on sharing the seamount's soul and his thoughts became crisp, his purpose defined, and his path obvious. Obvious, as the contrast between the arid desert and pristine white flakes that fell from the sunny blue sky.

Some heard, and many heard about, the seamount roaring that day. Its energy rocked the solemn flotilla hovering above it and as was his wish, Pepe felt the water again and dove the seamount.

# Chapter 50

It was summer now and whole families teeming with wanderlust had sailed south to the rustic villages. A fair share of Americans who had renounced the Americana of the Florida vacation, or even worse Hawaii, also made Baja their segregate home for a time. The gringos congealed on beach campsites along the two thousand mile coastline enjoying an isolated freedom unknown in America, save perhaps in the veil of cloistered national parks.

Baja attracted an odd lot of expatriates. They spilled onto the peninsula and trickled down to the deserted valleys and shores where the arid landscape absorbed them. Foreigners found it strange to believe how something so beautiful, so desolate, could exist just miles from the U.S. border. Fortunately God had smiled up the wild peninsula and spared it by keeping it free and wild. Accident or fate it really didn't matter, the main point was that throughout its relatively uninhabited history Baja remained isolated from a populous world that surrounded it.

According to the 1533 Spanish conquerors, the first inhabitants were native Baja Indians living in squalor on agrarian outposts. Cortez, as he was prone to do, arrived unfittingly enough in La Paz in 1535 and naturally claimed the land for Spain. And so it remained for several centuries until Mexico declared independence and of the original 50,000 or so Baja Indians all were wiped antiseptically off the face of the world; or so the Spaniards thought, for the blood of the Baja Indians seeped into the very land from wince it came.

The independence from Spain, however, brought Mexico into conflict with the unbridled expansionism of the United States. Unsuccessful first with a bid of

$3.5 million, then $40 million, the United States embarked on war. The warring countries eventually decided on peace, and Baja hung in the balance.

After the Spanish-American war, the United States ceded Baja along with what are today New Mexico, Arizona, and Texas. The peninsula's future dangled in the victor's hands, for the powers that be decreed that it was to become American war spoils. But for whatever reason, thankfully, America seemed satiated with reaching its manifest destiny through the annexation of the Southwest and discarded the wild peninsula under The Treaty of Gudalupe. So now the sun sets on the shores of two Mexican states, Baja California Norte and Baja California Sur, joined geographically but principally sovereign from the mainland, and indeed the world.

For many years Baja was the territory only for game fisherman and rambunctious youth in their quests to escape the United States. It is now a place where the Baja Mexicans enjoy a lifestyle freer and in suspiciously more affluent character than the mainland or America. Noticeably lacking in infrastructure and still shrouded in relative obscurity, Baja is the place where true freedom lives, indeed thrives.

0-595-32085-6

Printed in the United States
20847LVS00006B/460-486

9 780595 320851